The

J.S Ellis

All copyright © 2020 Joanne Saccasan All rights reserved. No part of this book may be used or reproduced in any way without permission except in the case of quotations or book reviews. This book is a work of fiction. Name, characters, businesses, organisations, places, events, locales and incidents are either the product of the author's imagination or used in a fictitious manner. Any resemblance to an actual person, living or dead, or actual events or locales is entirely coincidental.

For information contact:
Black Cat Ink Press
https://blackcatinkpress.com/
J.S Ellis
https://www.joannewritesbooks.com
Cover Design by: Milbart
Edited and proofread by: Edited by Melanie Underwood proofread by Red Pen Editor
ISBN: E book 978-99957-1-683-7
Paperback 978-99957-1-684-4
This book is written and edited in English

Chapter One

I stare at the laptop—an innocent little device, but not so innocent when it belonged to someone else. Someone who was a friend. Someone who is dead. I don't know what's in it; I haven't switched it on yet. I borrowed it from her and now she is dead. Murdered is the right word. Why Lottie? Her of all people? She died alone and helpless and the last face she saw before her final breath left her was of her killer. Tears roll down my cheeks. I crouch down and cover my face with my hands. I let it flood out of me. It hasn't sunk in yet—it's been a few days and still I can't believe it. Who would want Lottie dead? I wipe my tears away as if someone can see me. My forehead is moist with sweat while my brain works out what I can do. There are two possibilities:

Head to the police station and hand the laptop over. It's part of a murder investigation now, and the police are going to search for it. It belongs in an evidence bag with all the rest of her belongings.

Hand the laptop over after I see what is on it.

My laptop broke down and I had to do some designs; being the nice girl she was, Lottie offered to lend me hers. That was a week ago; three days later, she was dead. How had this happened?

Lottie didn't have enemies, at least not the kind who'd wish her dead. What am I going to do?

It creeps on me to switch the laptop on to see what's on it. It's about time the police came knocking. They must have gathered a basic list of who they need to speak to by now. It tears me apart knowing Lottie is gone forever, out of my life. All I have left are the memories of what we shared.

I turn on the gas; the cooker goes poof. I bend forwards, leaning my head closer to inhale. The gas fills my lungs and I explode in fits of coughs. What am I doing? I switch off the stove and look around my tiny kitchen with its blue walls. I find the colour serene and peaceful. It relaxes me. My kitchen is basic with a stove, a fridge and a few pots and pans hanging on the wall. A wooden table at the side. A window overlooking the backyard of the flat. The birds are singing and my neighbour, whose name I can't remember, is watering the plants. I cough again and I light a match, turning the cooker back on. Yellow flames come to life on the stove and I put the kettle on.

I emerge in the living room; it has coffee-coloured walls and a white ceiling. There are large bow windows, with red curtains and matching fitted carpet. I walk to the unused fireplace. On the cover are photos of me with Davian. My childhood friend. Davian and I work for the same company, Visage, an art company owned by Giselle Pearson

There are other photos of me taken in exhibitions and art galleries. I don't have any with Lottie. We didn't take pictures; now I wish we had.

I have all sorts of sculptures I made myself on the floor and on the furniture. The living room is cluttered with artistic stuff. I am a sculptor by profession, self-taught but took art in college. I spot a bottle of vodka, grab it by the neck, unscrew the top and take a large gulp. The liquid swooshes down my throat, making my chest burn as if it's set on fire. I wipe my mouth on my sleeve and pull a disgusted face. I was never a big fan of vodka.

I sit in front of the desk and stare down at the laptop. What's on it scares me. All I have to do is switch it on. I have the password. Lottie had given it to me, and it's saved on my phone. I see what's on it and find a way to give it to the police. I exhale and take out a cigarette from its packet with a trembling hand. I can almost feel her presence, Lottie placing her hand on my shoulder. I glance back with a hope and I see her smiling down at me, but no one is there. I rub my face with my hands and light the cigarette. If I give this to the police once I'm done, will they run it for prints? The kettle screams in the kitchen. The chair scrapes on the floor as I rise. I shut the kettle up and start to open drawers and cupboards. So much shit; do I really need all these utensils? How did this piece of clay get here?

I find a pair of yellow washing-up gloves in the cupboard under the sink. My cigarette has turned to ash. I kindle another. I catch my reflection from the screen, my wavy longish dark hair, golden skin tone, green hazel eyes and heart-shaped face.

I press the power button and the laptop comes to life, ready to hit me with whatever it contains.

Maybe, I'm fussing over nothing. I input the password and wait for it to boot. The home screen appears for a moment, and I think a picture of her might appear. I don't think I can take it, seeing her picture right now. To my relief, it's a scene of a beach somewhere. I'm guessing Thailand. Lottie always said she wanted to go there. It's a shame the only glimpse of Thailand she had is from a desktop. Her toes will never touch the sand and the sun will never kiss her skin.

It feels wrong doing this, snooping over my friend's computer; it's like I'm invading her privacy. She wouldn't know but still, it doesn't feel right.

I don't think she used this laptop a lot. Judging from its appearance, it's in mint condition. I take a deep breath as I move the console to her emails; nothing looks important. Spam, junk mail and offers from online shops. Boring stuff. Next, I go the folder titled *Photos* and they start to load one by one. I lower my head and my eyes start to water. It's too painful, the wounds are too fresh. Why am I doing this? I have to do this. I must do this. I need to do this. This laptop is the only link I have left of her, the only connection between us. I have to find out what happened and this laptop might have something that might lead to a clue to why she was killed. I can't think of anyone who would want her dead. Lottie was a quiet, reserved girl, who didn't bother anyone and no one bothered her. She had me and Ella as her friends and people at work liked her. She had a good relationship with her parents. Never did drugs or slept around and drank to the bare minimum. She had boyfriends, some good, and some bad. Nothing too dramatic, and then there was him. Davian. Lottie always had been fascinated with him. She thought he was the prettiest man she had ever seen. Lottie worked with him. I can call Davian, but I don't want to be around people.

I skip the photos for now and go to her documents. There is one single folder. I click on it and it asks me for the password. I blink at the screen. What did Lottie have to hide that needed a password? Nude photos of herself? So, when years have gone by, she could look at them to see what a knockout she was? A sex tape? What?
I type Lottie Gibson.
Nothing.
Her mobile number.
Nothing happens.
I type my name for the hell of it.
No success.
I huff, giving up. Something has to be important in that folder if she felt the need to have it password protected. I click on videos. I catch my breath as a set of videos start to load. My blood goes cold and my muscles tense as I move the console to the first video clip titled 'one', the last clip is titled 'fifteen'. The first clip was uploaded a year ago and the last clip two weeks ago. I press the play button and her face comes alive before me. I slip off the chair and land on my arse as her voice fills the room. What kind of fucked-up shit is this?

I get up, stop the video. I grip my hair with my fingers. I shiver as tears sting my eyes. I get up and look out the window to distract myself from this discovery. It's a beautiful Monday morning and the sun is out with cumulus humilis clouds in the blue sky. The same woman from across the street is preparing her son for school. A man comes out from the next block holding a briefcase. He waves to the woman and says something to her son. Do these people care my friend is dead? How can they prepare their kids to school or go to work and wave at each other and say good morning? When the most important thing is Lottie's death. What's more important than her death right now?

People die and life goes on. Soon, I have to do the same, move on and get on with my life and all I have is a collection of memories of her. Would I ever heal from this? I pass by the bottle of vodka I abandoned earlier. I cough as this tasteless, odourless drink hugs my body.

I smoke and pace around the room, avoiding looking at the laptop. Why did she lend it to me? Did she do it intentionally? Most importantly, what was she trying to achieve by making those videos?

I take out my headphones from my backpack. I take a deep breath and press play.

***

Lottie's Recordings
I know why I'm doing this. There are things you can't tell your family or friends. Some things

are best kept to yourself, but what happens when you can't take it anymore? When they start to eat you out? What happens then? Do you keep on going until they drive you mad? I think I'm going mad.

***

Was she in danger? Is this why she made those videos? I stare at her lovely face. How the sun used to shine on her long brown wavy hair. Her thick eyebrows complemented her heart-shaped face and her strong cheekbones. How she used to look at me with her big almond-shaped grey-blue eyes. The way she used to press her bee-sting lips together before she spoke. Her milky white skin free from blemishes. There was something innocent and mysterious about her, but it was a beautiful face.

I press pause. Is this what these videos are? A trip to memory lane? So she would look back in years and laugh at herself? I let it pour out of me, why her? Why did it have to be her? Why would someone do this? What had she done to deserve this? Why was she the one to suffer?

The buzzer makes me jump as it pierces through the silence. I rise from the chair and go to the window; there is a man with black hair and a woman with red hair. They must be detectives; they had to be.

Chapter Two

The panic rises as I snatch the laptop off the desk and survey the room. This is my home. It's safe and secure, but nowhere seems to be safe enough to hide this computer, not with what it contains. I open the cupboard under the sink and place it with the washing detergents. The buzzer slices through the flat again. I open a garbage bag and seal the laptop in it. Not the best hiding place, but it will do for now.

I take a deep breath and I buzz the detectives in without speaking to them through the intercom. The woman is attractive, in her forties with delicate features, green eyes and flaming red hair. The man has short black hair, dark eyes and thin lips. They have their badges ready, but I don't peek at their IDs.

'Good morning,' the man says. 'I'm DC James Taylor and this is my partner DC Fiona Gallagher. Are you Anthony Hughes?'

'Yes.'

Still holding his badge, he says, 'We would like to ask you a few questions regarding Lottie Gibson. We're sorry for your loss.'

I glance at their IDs and lead the way. They look at each other and proceed inside. The woman scans the flat, looking at my designs, my record collection and books.

'You're an artist?' DC Gallagher asks, looking at the picture on the wall.

It's an artwork of a nude woman given to me by Davian.

'No, a sculptor,' I say.

'How old are you?' DC Gallagher asks, now eyeing me.

I maintain eye contact with her. 'Twenty-five.'

DC Taylor takes out his notebook and pen. 'How long did you know the victim?'

I sit across from him on the armchair. 'Three years.'

He scribbles on the notebook. 'Would you say you're close?'

'Yes, we were close.'

'And you were the one who found her job for...' he flips pages of his notebook, 'Giselle Pearson?'

I work for Giselle. Well, sort of. She buys the sculptures from me and she sells them. Her company sells photographs and sculptures from artists and photographers. Giselle is always hungry for new talent. For the next best thing. She owns a gallery, dealing with the *crème de la crème* in the city. Davian is her main photographer and collaborator; to put it bluntly, her leading man. I thought working with Giselle would help Lottie get back on her feet after she got laid off from her previous job.

'Yes, I did. I had a word with Giselle to see if there were any openings. She was looking for an assistant, doing coffees, photocopies, filing, that sort of thing.'

DC Taylor nods. 'Her ex-boyfriend, Abdel - did she talk to you about him?'

I light a cigarette. 'Not a lot, but she seemed happy with him. He treated her well, took her out to fancy restaurants, surprised her, and they went on trips together.'

'She never mentioned he was violent or treated her with disrespect?' DC Gallagher asks.

Do they think Abdel is involved in her murder? How could he be when they broke up months ago?

'No, she didn't.'

DC Taylor looks down at his notepad.

'Did she mention another man in the picture or give you the impression she was seeing someone?'

Another man in the picture? Where are they going with this? Are they implying that Lottie was seeing someone in secret?

I blink at him. 'You mean in secret?' I ask.

'We're the ones asking the questions,' DC Gallagher points out.

'It wouldn't surprise me.'

Dc Taylor lifts an eyebrow. 'What do you mean it wouldn't surprise you?'

'Well... she's a pretty girl,' I say.

DC Taylor rests his back on the sofa. 'Yes, she was a beautiful girl.'

'Why did she break off with her boyfriend?' DC Gallagher asks.

I place the cigarette on the ashtray and shift on my seat.

'He was the one who broke up with her the first time.'

'When was this?' DC Gallagher asks.

I stretch my neck. 'There was a work party and Lottie brought Abdel as her date.'

'Were you at this party?' she asks.

'Yes, I was. Abdel was talking to Davian and—'

'Davian Levine?' DC Taylor asks, checking his notebook for clarification.

'Yes.'

'He's Lottie's colleague, correct?' DC Taylor asks.

'Yes.'

'How long have you known him?' DC Gallagher said, her eyes never leaving me.

I play with my lighter. 'Since childhood.'

'What happened at the party?' DC Gallagher asks.

'As I said, Abdel and Davian were engaged in a deep discussion. Lottie began wrapping her arms around me and my date wasn't too happy about that.'

'What about Abdel?' DC Taylor asks.

'They left. I found out later that he broke up with her.'

'Did she tell you the reason behind the breakup?'

I run my hand through my hair. 'She said Davian said something to him.'

'Do you remember what he said?'

'Something about us being too close, that there was something going on between us, which wasn't true.'

It came back to me that day; Davian didn't feel any remorse for what he did, but that's him:

stubborn. A complication of being an artist, he likes to call it. I call it being an ass.

'Did Lottie have any enemies, someone who wished her harm?' DC Gallagher took over the questioning.

I shake my head. 'No, she had no enemies.'

'And her relationship with her colleagues was good?'

'Yes...'

I glanced at them, those two detectives sitting on my sofa. DC Taylor scribbling in his notebook, DC Gallagher analysing me, maybe to see if I had a motive to kill her. In the kitchen cupboard is Lottie's laptop; I'm sure they are wondering if she owned one. I don't think they've established that yet, but they will. They need to go through her social media, her emails and documents, anything that can help with the investigation. I'm safe. Nobody knows she lent me her laptop except her, and Lottie isn't going to talk. Perhaps they will suspect that the killer took it. I want to ask how did she die? If she suffered? Was her death slow or quick?

'Can I get a glass of water?' I ask.

'Please do,' DC Taylor says.

I rise and go into the kitchen, wash a dirty glass from the sink and put it under the tap. Do they think I have something to do with her death? They can check; I was in the exhibition that Giselle had set up. There are security footage and hundreds of guests to confirm it. My alibi is solid. She is dead.

Gone. I take a deep breath, refill the glass and take it with me to the sitting room.

'Where were you the night she was killed?' DC Taylor asks.

I sit down. 'I was at an exhibition Giselle had organised. My work was displayed in there.'

DC Taylor nods and scribbles in his notebook.

DC Gallagher rubs her hands together as if she's cold. 'How did you and Lottie meet?'

'I met Lottie at a party. A friend of a friend introduced us. She was quite distant, really sad. She had just broken up with a boyfriend she had been dating on and off.'

'And who was this ex-boyfriend' DC Taylor asked.

'Jackie... I can't remember his surname... um... Robinson, yes, that's it, Jackie Robinson. We talked about the mishap with her ex. She seemed all over the place. I met her about two months later. A friend of hers hosted another party at her house. I was invited, she was there. We met up a few times after that with other friends then we decided to meet alone as we had a lot in common.'

The memories haunt me. We used to go to the park, sit on a bench and talk as life went by around us.

I lower my head.

'Are you all right?' DC Gallagher asks gently.

'She was rather naive about certain things,' I said, my voice cracking. 'She would rush into things and believed in love. She wanted to be loved and she was loved.'

Only she didn't know it, I would never get the chance to tell her how I truly felt about her and now it's too late.

Chapter Three

'Thank you for your time,' DC Gallagher says.

She takes out a card from her jacket pocket and hands it to me. 'If you think of something, anything at all, please, do not hesitate to call.'

I take her card. It's plain white with her name, surname, and her number in bold. Under her details, 24/7 is written neatly with a blue softball pen. If it were a different place, on a different day, I would have laughed, but this isn't the time or place, and if it were any other day, I would never have crossed paths with this detective.

From the kitchen window, I watch them get in the car but they don't drive off right away. I think they're discussing what I told them. Planning who they should talk to next. A few minutes later, the black sedan drives away. I kneel down on the floor and open the cupboard. I take out the laptop from the garbage bag. Such a dangerous possession to own. I can go to prison for this. The police didn't say how Lottie died. I will find out one way or another, and I will not rest until I do.

I take out a piece of paper and pen and I write down the names of the people I have to talk to. People who knew Lottie. Her parents, Ella and Abdel. There are her work colleagues Lilia, Giselle and Davian. I need to do this without attracting too much attention to myself. I also need to track the locations she had been in the last few days of her life. I open drawers and cupboards, searching for a map with no luck. I pack the laptop in my backpack along with the list of names.

The cold bites me as I step out and I button up my jacket. A motorcycle rumbles in my ears. A man in a brown coat flies past me, nearly hitting me with his briefcase. I stop at the ATM and withdraw some cash to buy a map from the gift shop. I could use the map on my phone, but I need to mark the locations. London howls and screams around me. The crowds of people talking on their phones; nobody gives a damn about one other. All they care about is to get on with their day. I descend the stairs to the tube, and a girl behind me is talking to her friend about a man she met. They laugh as they scuttle past me to the newsagent.

Some cases hardly make headlines, but this one does. There is a picture of Lottie. She's smiling prettily at the camera. The press must have taken it from her Facebook. They sure work fast.

Young woman found dead in her apartment.

Lottie Gibson, 25, was found dead by her landlord after tenants complained about loud music coming from her apartment at midnight last night. There were no signs of a break-in or a struggle.

The last time the victim was seen alive was on Saturday evening, leaving a restaurant with a friend. Lottie worked as an assistant in an art company called *Visage* owned by Giselle Pearson. No statements have been released yet.

Lottie was having dinner with Ella before she got killed. Ella was the last person who saw her alive. She would be able to provide information about Lottie in the final hours of her life. For the police, this would be one of those cases that would be solved in a matter of days unless it gets more complicated. If Lottie was found dead in her apartment, then she must have let the killer in. It had to be someone she knew. Who? The killer must have put the music on to muffle the screams.

In the tube, I find an empty seat and I unfold the map. I inspect the locations. The sushi restaurant called Ikedia is in Mayfair, the last place Lottie had been. I draw a circle in Sutton where Lottie's apartment was. I mark another circle in Richmond, her parents' house. Along with Promise Hill, Ella's place, Leadenhall Street where the offices and the art gallery are. Greenwich where Abdel lives, and Camden, my place.

I send Ella a text asking her if she's at work. A reply comes right away with a no and how about I come over for a cup of tea?

Ella is a fresh-faced girl. I can describe her as the girl next door when it comes to looks. There is something classic about her. Maybe it is the oval face or the high cheekbones, or perhaps her almond-shaped, deep-set blue eyes. Her hair is blonde, cut in a bob which has a hint of waves.

'I just can't...' Ella trails off.

She takes out a tissue from her jeans pocket and blows her nose. I wipe my tears away with my thumb and forefinger and we walk inside the house. The scent of vanilla hits my nostrils. I notice the candle has burned to the bottom. There are several photographs on the maple table by the white leather sofa. Ella is an assistant in fashion shows; it's quite a glamorous job, or at least, I think it is. There are photographs on the wall from fashion shows. The one that stands out is with Belle. Belle is the ex-girlfriend of Abdel; he's a photographer and she's a popular model. She appeared in a string of well-known magazines such as *Elle*, *Vanity Fair* and *Vogue*.

In the photograph, Ella is wearing a tight-fitting t-shirt with the word 'Beauty' in fuchsia and an arrow pointing at Belle. Belle was wearing a light pink silk robe and a black lace bra, her dark hair tied in a sleek ponytail. There is another photo with Lottie, neither are looking at the camera but laughing at something. I will never again hear the sound of her laugh, and how her face lit up when she smiled. There is a suitcase by the sofa. Ella walks into the spotless white kitchen and puts the kettle on. She turns, facing me, and fires up a cigarette. I notice her hands are trembling.

'Did the police talk to you?' she asks.

'Yes.'

'I can't believe we were sitting across from each other eating sushi, laughing and having a good time.'

'I know it's...' I pause, trying to put it into words. 'I can't describe it... Did the police tell you how she...?'

Ella shakes her head 'No, they didn't. I think they told her parents and that's it. There isn't much in the papers either.'

'Ella, the detectives asked me if Lottie was seeing another man besides Abdel. Did she tell you she was seeing someone?'

Her eyebrows rise. 'No, she didn't say. It came as much of a shock to me as it is to you.'

The kettle boils.

Ella switches off the gas. 'Are you the guy she was meeting secretly?'

I stare at her, taken aback by her crude question. Did she just ask if I was having an affair with Lottie?

I shake my head. 'No, I wasn't. I can't believe you would ask me something like that.'

Ella turns to me. 'Well, I always wondered how you two remained friends; you were cute together. I always thought you'll end up a couple.'

I smile. 'Nah, I respected her too much.'

She opens the top cupboard. 'That's the point. You would have made her very happy, Anthony.'

'So, the police think there is another man?' I ask, changing the subject.

She takes two mugs from the cupboard. 'I think so. Do you think Abdel is a suspect?'

'They broke up months ago. I don't think they kept in touch, considering how things ended between them,' I say, running my thumb over the plastic tablecloth.

Ella hands me my mug which has *'I'm in fashion, bitch'* engraved in gold. She reaches for her packet of cigarettes and offers me one as she sits across from me.

'Have you spoken to her parents?'

'No, not yet.'

'Gosh. The poor parents.'

I took a sip of tea—it's strong but good. 'Do you think the guy she was seeing was married?'

'Could be,' Ella says.

'It's not like her to have an affair.'

She rubs the back of her head. 'You never know with people.'

'Did she tell you where she was going afterwards?'

Ella looks at me as if I'm insane. 'She said she was going to see you.'

I blink at her. 'What?'

'You had the exhibition, right? Lottie said she was going to drop by and say hello.'

There were lots of faces in the exhibition, but I would never miss hers. If Lottie came to see me, why didn't she talk to me? Because she didn't come to the exhibition. It was a lie. Lottie went somewhere else or met with someone. Someone who might have been her killer.

Ella stares at me. 'She didn't come to the exhibition?'

'No, she didn't. I would have seen her... I mean she would have spoken to me.'

Ella curls her lip. 'Strange. Maybe she said that to me but went to meet this man…' She pauses and sighs, exasperated. 'I don't know.'

'Did you tell the police she was coming to see me?'

Ella leans her back on the chair. 'No, I forgot. I was too shocked by the news to recall every single detail.'

It made sense Lottie would lie to Ella to meet this man. Maybe she met him at her place. Maybe this man went there with the intention to kill her, or maybe there was an argument which got out of hand and he killed her. One thing is certain, if Lottie lied to Ella, then she lied to me too.

Chapter Four

I slump on a secluded bench in Regent's Park. It isn't as crowded - there are people laying on the grass reading, others strolling by. I look to my left and right before unzipping my bag and taking out the laptop. I hook in the headphones since those videos were private; Lottie might have mentioned an affair or a man she had been seeing. I scrolled down the videos - this was going to take time. I go back to the protected file, tapping my fingers. Lottie had secrets like everyone else, a part of me doesn't want to crack the password. What if there is something I'd rather not know?

I type 'chocolate cake', one of her obsessions.

No luck.

I shut my eyes, taking a deep breath, and she comes to life before me.

***

Lottie's Recordings. Clip One

Adulthood is so complicated; it starts when you turn eighteen. When you come to an age where you don't belong to your mother anymore, but to yourself and to the world. Here I am, open and exposed, but nobody warned me of anything; I had to find out for myself. I wish I could just crawl back into my childhood where I was afraid of the dark. Parents tell stories, sometimes dark ones, to frighten us. When you grow up, you realise those stories were not true. Maybe it was their way to warn us of what's to come.

I'm scared shitless. I don't know anything about art and out of the goodness of his heart, Anthony has arranged for me to meet his boss.

I used to work with a small importing company until it was shut down, and all I had was a letter of recommendation and a mind swimming with worries. The bills were piling up and the rent was due.

***

The day Lottie was made redundant, she showed up at my door, all upset and crying.

'What am I going to do?' she asked.

She was so fragile and sometimes, it made me want to shake her and tell her to grow a pair. This is life: you take a stumble and you pick yourself up. No use crying about it; it won't fix anything. You'll remain unemployed with bills to pay and the landlord knocking on your door demanding the rent. Update your resume, start applying for jobs, go to interviews - you have to keep on going. Of course, I didn't tell her any of this. I would have come across as insensitive and uncaring.

'Don't worry, everything is going to be fine,' I said, sitting across from her, handing her a cup of tea.

'How can you say that? I'm about to lose my apartment!' she snapped, tears smearing down her face. 'I have about a month left for rent then I have to move out and I love that apartment.'

I handed her a box of Kleenex. 'I'll speak to my boss. I think she has openings.'

Lottie looked at me with wide, bloodshot eyes. 'Your boss? But she runs an art company? I don't know anything about art!'

'Nothing like that, I think she's looking for an assistant.'

I thought the job would fit her. More glamorous than an export company.

'Everything will be all right,' I assured her.

She started filming these videos during the time she started working for Giselle, a year ago. That job is where everything started. I regret it, to be honest, going to Giselle and asking her if she had any job openings. That's when the trouble started.

Giselle loved Lottie. She had plans for her, and the news of her death must have blown her away. The first video clip finishes with her saying she had the interview.

I go back to my map. I mark Westminster where Davian lives. How does Davian feel about this? I dial his number, but the call goes straight to voicemail. I think about going to his apartment but I change my mind.

Chapter Five
Lottie's Recordings. Clip Two

I was forty-five minutes early; the building wasn't far from the Leadenhall Building. I found a café called The Breakfast Club. That's also my favourite movie, so, I took it as a sign of good fate. I sat by the window and ordered a cup of coffee, browsed through the menu, although the thought of food made my stomach flip. The place wasn't busy: a couple eating their lunch quietly, a man sitting alone with a pile of files, and a tourist, Spanish I think.

Anthony never told me what Giselle was like and his best friend, Davian, worked there too. I never met this Davian. His name did pop up occasionally, but I'd never met him in person, which was strange; this was Anthony's best friend and he'd never introduced us.

***

The right time never came up. Davian travelled a lot, to Japan and Indonesia mostly, and I didn't think it mattered much them meeting. I wasn't preventing them; I'm sure they would have met at some point. She knew he worked there as I'm sure she had googled Davian and now she was going to meet him. Like me, Davian worked from home mostly, but since he's Giselle's main man, he has to show his face there more than I do.

***

The waiter brought me my coffee. Meanwhile, I googled the company. There was a picture of a stunning black woman in her forties. Giselle. She worked in art galleries and had vast experience in photography. She founded the company six years ago with a businessman who had no experience in art, and she bought him out three years ago. Giselle now runs the company; there are thirty people working for her. The concept is finding new talent and displaying their art or photos in her own art gallery.

The Spanish tourist stood to leave. That was when I took real notice of him, the man sitting alone on the table with a few folders scattered on the table. He sipped on his coffee, his eyes never leaving the documents. His hair was immaculately styled. He seemed like the kind of man who took care of his appearance. He was dressed in a black suit along with a crisp white shirt and a tie which had sequins on it. He flipped the page and I noticed they weren't documents, but photographs. I sipped my coffee as I continued to marvel at the man. He didn't look any older than I was.

He ran his hand over his perfect, starlight blond hair. It was cut in firefly wedge style but messier. A flick fell on his forehead, covering his left eye. It had to be him, I thought. I opened my browser on my phone and typed Davian Levin. There wasn't much information about him.

As if he knew what I was doing, he looked up and I was hit with a pair of icy blue eyes piercing through my soul. The cup slipped, causing the liquid to splash on my hand. The hotness stung. I pushed the chair back as anxiety and panic swept over me. To my dismay, there was a large stain on my shirt. The waiter rushed over with napkins.

"I'll bring you another,' he said, referring to the coffee.

'Where is the bathroom?' I asked, my eyes moist with tears.

I was on my way for an interview with an important woman, in some fancy arty place, and I'm about to show up with coffee stains on my shirt because I got distracted by some random hot guy.

In the bathroom, I tried to fix my shirt as much as I could. I took it off and applied soap on it. I cried as I rubbed the shirt furiously. A woman walked in and gave me an odd look and went in the cubical. The stain wasn't completely gone but it wasn't as visible as before. I retouched my make-up and slipped out of the bathroom. The waiter had cleared the table and there was a fresh cup of coffee. Davian was back at his photographs. I tried not to stare, but my eyes couldn't help it. He was so glamorous. So stylish and elegant. I had fifteen minutes left and the nerves were making me sweat. The butterflies in my stomach increased. 'It's just an interview' I kept telling myself. If I don't get the job, it won't be the end of the world. I had been to interviews before and hadn't fussed this much. But since Anthony had arranged this, I wanted him to be proud of me.

After I paid, I felt Davian's eyes on me. I took a final glance at him. He had an eyebrow raised but it was arched that way. He had delicate facial features, almost feminine, sharp cheekbones, fair skin, chiselled jawline, and those cold blue eyes.

When I entered the building, I was swallowed by fashionable looking people. It was like Chanel meeting Andy Warhol. 'Anthony works with those people?' I thought, but he's so laid back and easy going. These people looked so stuck up.

My heart thumped against my chest as I walked into a marbled reception with white walls. Behind the desk stood a well-dressed man who gave me a pass and told me where to go. I located the lift. I will never get this job. I don't fit in. I'm not like these people. I'm a jeans girl and if I do get the job, I'll have to reinvent my wardrobe, and I don't have that kind of money to spend. I came across another reception. This reception had a grey fitted carpet and white walls with a huge photograph of a woman's back in black and white. The furniture was part maple, part white, and I could see the offices since the walls were glass. Sexy chill-out house music played. It gave the office an atmosphere of a fancy lounge bar. The heavily made-up girl behind the desk pouted at the screen. She had blonde hair pushed back in a bun and wore a navy suit. The phone rang and after she hung up, she stood and escorted me to a glass office. Giselle stood behind her desk. She was about six feet tall and looked even better in real life, like a model with strong features and a sheet of glossy dark hair.

'Lottie, so wonderful to meet you,' she said, smiling pleasantly.

She seemed nice. Perhaps since my nerves were screaming across her prestigious office, she felt sorry for me, and wanted to make me feel comfortable instead of laughing me out of the building.

'Thank you for having me, Ms Pearson,' I said.

She smiled gesturing at one of her guest chairs. 'Would you like some tea or coffee?'

'Coffee, please,' I said.

Her office was sleek like the rest of the place; a large photograph of a woman's torso hung on the wall. A white sofa with purple cushions and a coffee table. On top of it was a purple curved ruby dragon tea set that must have cost an arm and leg. Her desk was clean and organised with a small laptop, a notepad and an expensive-looking pen.

'One tea and one coffee,' she said to the blonde.

After the blonde left, leaving the door open, Giselle sat across from me. I tried not to stare but this woman was remarkable. She seemed like someone I could look up to. Strong but feminine, powerful even.

'So, you're Anthony's friend?' she asked.

I squeezed my knees together. 'Yes,'

'Not his girlfriend?' She arched an eyebrow.

I shook my head. 'No.'

'Talented young man.'

'Yes, he is,' I said, nodding gravely.

'Since you are friends with Anthony, you must know Davian?'

I pushed a strand of hair behind my ear. I thought of the man I have seen at the café and his icy stare.

'No, I've never met him.'

For a moment, I thought she was going to call him. How awkward it would be, interviewed by Anthony's best friend who I'd never met. The blonde receptionist wiggled her way into the office with a tray. She placed it on Giselle's desk and left without closing the door behind her. Giselle placed an expensive china cup in front of me.

'So, tell me,' Giselle said, 'why do you want this job?'

Oh God, here it comes. The same tedious tiresome questions. The money, I need the money. I haven't done any intensive research on the company except at the coffee shop. I felt like an unprepared idiot.

'Well... I'm a fast learner and I make a mean cup of tea,' I blurted.

Giselle smiled. 'Do you have any experience in art?'

'No.'

'Photography?'

I shift my bottom on the chair in discomfort. 'No.'

'But you've worked as an assistant before?'

'Yes.'

'What did you do there?'

'Answer the phone, email clients. Filing, I did bookkeeping, set up appointments for my boss...'

'The job here is different. I already have a personal assistant. What I need is someone who is fast at getting things done. You'll do the filing, I have a room which needs clearing, and you wouldn't be dealing with phones or bookkeeping. I have people who are qualified to do that. I need someone to set up the gallery downstairs, run errands, and take care of the stationery. You will also be assisting Davian, my main photographer and business partner. You will meet him now since Anthony failed to do so. He's my star.'

I'd be assisting Davian? With what? Davian is her partner? So technically, he'll be my boss.

I lifted the cup. 'So, Davian will be my boss?'

She gave me a stern look. 'No, I'm your boss. Don't forget that.'

'Okay.'

'Some gallery openings are held at weekends. Would that be a problem?'

'No.'

'Long hours?'

'No.'

'Excellent. Since Anthony spoke so highly of you and you seem like a bright, sensible girl, you'll start on Monday.'

I wanted to jump up, clap my hands together and hug her, but I remained composed. 'Thank you.'

We discussed my salary as we sipped our coffees. As I was telling her about my years in college, there was a knock on the door.

'Ah, just in time,' Giselle said, standing.

I did a double take, nearly dropping the china cup. Davian strode in. He didn't seem to notice I was there. But why would he? I was invisible, at least to him. He talked about his photographs, which sounded so strange and foreign to me.

'We'll talk about that later, Davian. There is someone I would like you to meet,' Giselle said, placing her hand on his forearm.

I bet he recognised me, but he didn't bat an eyelid. He seemed so pompous, so snotty. Like someone who took himself way too seriously. I jumped as his eyes passed through me like lasers.

'This is Lottie. She's Anthony's friend, and she's going to start here on Monday.'

He smiled politely and reached out a hand. I wobbled on my feet. I took his hand; it was warm and his handshake was firm. I kept on staring at him lost in a trance. He smelled good too. Chanel, I presumed.

'How come I never met you before?' he said in a deep soothing voice.

'I don't know. You have to ask him.'

'Strange guy, that Anthony. Send him my regards.'

I felt my cheeks colour. 'Oh... of course.'

Giselle had her hands across her chest, eyeing us. This is Anthony's friend and he had been hiding him all this time!

'Lottie, be here at nine o'clock sharp and ask for Lilia. She will show you the ropes,' Giselle said.

'Yes, thank you.'

I took one last glance at Davian, but he didn't smile or say anything. I turned to take my leave.

'And I take your word for it,' Giselle added.

I turned to face them. They looked so powerful and beautiful while I was the cockroach who'd made its way to this classy building.

'For the mean cup of tea,' Giselle said, and winked.

'Oh, anytime. Bye.'

Chapter Six

I stop at the reception. Lilia glances up at me and rises from her chair and rushes over to hug me.

'My God, I can't believe it.'

'Me neither. Is Giselle in?'

'Yes, she's in.'

'Thanks.'

'I might have to talk to you later,' I tell her.

'Yes, of course, when?' she asks.

'I'll call you....'

Giselle is behind her desk working on her laptop or, checking for updates regarding the murder. That reminds me, I need to check what the newspapers are saying. Maybe something new had come up. I knock on the door.

'Anthony.' Giselle stands, opening her arms. 'Darling, I'm so sorry.'

We embrace for a few seconds then I pull away.

'Who would do this?' she says, rubbing her hands on my arms.

'I don't know.'

'Please, have a seat. Would you like something to drink?'

'No, I'm fine,' I say.

Giselle sits down across from me. 'Lottie was such a sweet, beautiful young woman. Who would want to harm her?'

'I don't know.'

'The detectives were here. They came this morning. They seemed particularly interested in Davian and for the life of me I don't know why.'

My eyebrows lift to my forehead. 'Were they?'

'Yes, they asked me about his working relationship with Lottie.'

Why would the police be interested in Davian?

'What did you tell them?' I ask.

'What is there to tell?'

Is she covering his arse? I know she favours him because his photographs sell like hotcakes, and he brings her a lot of money, but there are limits.

'He's not an easy person to work with,' I point out. 'When was the last time you saw Lottie?' I ask.

'Four days ago.'

'How was she?'

'She was fine. Her usual self. Quiet, going about with her business.' Giselle keeps staring at me as if she could read me. 'Don't you go do anything stupid now.'

'I'm only trying to find out what happened.'

'I know you cared about her, we all did, but let the police handle it and focus on yourself.'

'She's my friend.'

'I know, I had hopes for her. So much potential.'

'Will it be okay if I...' I trailed off.

Her eyes shot at me. 'No need to ask. Take all the time you need.'

She opens a drawer, hands me an envelope and slips it across the desk. 'Take care and if you need anything, anything at all, you know where to find me.'

I stand to leave then I turn to her. 'Did you speak to Davian?'

'Yes, he's here,' she says, 'in his office.'

I knock on the frosted glass door where Davian's name is engraved in silver letters. A figure walks to the door and he appears before me. His office is not a glass box like Giselle's. I remember, he was specific about that. He didn't want anyone to look in and see what he was doing.

There is a dreamy quality about Davian, a combination of innocence, fragility and sadness upon his face that gives him a rather moody look. And he is moody, but there is something about him that even I have to admit myself is striking. He has a lot of female admirers, open to his affections. While this would stroke any man's ego, Davian has a frosty persona and he dismisses those female admirers as if they were rats; what might be surprising to some is that he doesn't see himself as good looking. Which makes him rather modest.

'Hey… I've heard… I'm shocked… I mean… it's….' he stalls, searching for the word, 'bad.'

From all the words he could have chosen, unspeakable, unbelievable, terrible, but no, he went for bad.

'I called you,' I say.

'You did? When?' he asks.

'Yesterday, in the afternoon.'

'I might have been driving Melissa to the airport.' He opens the door wider.

There are a set of beautiful pictures on the wall. Davian photographs landscapes and ordinary people, never models. He doesn't want to be associated with any of that. On the other hand, Melissa, his girlfriend, does artwork for bands and photographs celebrities and models. There is a glass table in the middle of the room, a laptop and different models of digital cameras and photographs in black and white scattered around it.

'How are you holding up?' he asks.

'Barely.'

He gestures at the chair for me to sit. 'Who would want to murder her?'

'I don't know.'

'The police came here asking me questions.'

'I know, Giselle told me.'

'They asked me all sort of baffling questions like what was my relationship with her. I didn't have a relationship with her; we were work colleagues. I wasn't associated with her outside this office,' he says in a stern and annoyed tone.

'Maybe someone talked about how you were with her,' I point out.

He stares at me coldly, his jaw clenched. 'How I was with her?'

'You know...'

'No, I don't,' he says.

I rub my eyes with my hands. 'Look, Davian. I didn't come here with any grudges or anything like that. I'm going through something that nobody can understand. To you, she might have been a silly girl with a crush who worked here, but to me, she was more than that.'

'Of course,' he says. 'Is there anything you need?'

'I need answers to why her? And who killed her?'

'That's the police's job, not yours.'

What disturbs me is how cool he is about the murder.

'Why didn't you call when you heard the news?' I ask, trying to mask the accusation in my voice.

He ponders on this. 'I figured you wanted your own space. I would have called you, but I wanted you to take your time. You know how I am.'

'Yes, I do know,' I say, 'I'm sorry, I'm not feeling myself.'

'Well, that's understandable. You are going through something traumatic. I'm here for you, remember that.'

Do I really want to know how she got killed? It's devastating enough as it is.

***

Lottie's Recordings. Clip Three

Today was my first day. I had mixed feelings about it. I know it's the first day, but your instinct tells you if you are going to like working there or not. There I stood with my outfit from Primark in the room full of Gucci. The place screamed at me,

'Get out you don't belong here!' I was so out of place.

A woman with red hair approached me, dressed in a beige pencil skirt, a red blouse and high heels.

She held out her hand. 'Hi, I'm Lilia. You must be Lottie.'

'Hi.'

'Shall we?' she asked, gesturing at the corridor after we exchanged pleasantries.

As we walked along the corridor, Davian was in one of the offices, talking to a man. He glanced at me but didn't smile or nod. No sign of recognition as if he hadn't see me at all. Instead he turned his attention back to the man.

'Forget it, honey,' Lilia said, catching me ogling.

'What?' I said, heat rising through my entire body and colouring my face.

'You have to wait in line. Ask any woman in this place - if they are stuck in a boat and they had to choose between a packet of digestive biscuits, a bottle of water, or him, most of them will say him. Besides, he's taken. Between you and me, he's too pretty for my liking. I like my man with an edge - manly, you know.'

I didn't know what to say. She escorted me to a room at the back where the cubicles were. There were six people: four women and two men typing on their keyboards and answering the phones. She introduced me to everyone. I didn't remember all of their names; I'm terrible with that. Lilia showed me where things were and where the kitchen was. Afterward, she took me to the room where I'll be working in the upcoming weeks. It was a room with four glass walls with boxes piled on top of each other. They had colour-coded Post-its and a row of cabinets at the end.

'Now, this is the room you'll be working in. As you can see, it's a mess and it's your job to make it all nice and tidy.'

'Me?'

'Yes, you.'

Of course they give the new girl the job nobody wants to do.

'Enjoy,' Lilia cooed. 'Call me if you'll get stuck, okay, sweetie?'

I spent the whole day filing, following the instructions on the Post-its. During my half an hour break, I sat outside the building eating a sandwich. I left at nine o'clock at night. I didn't mind; I had no other engagements.

****

Lottie had complained to me several times about the first few weeks when she started there. I think she was lucky she got the job in the first place. It paid the bills, after all. I thought it was a bit ungrateful, to be honest.

Chapter Seven

I stand in front of the blue door, holding a bouquet of flowers. I puff nervously, building the courage to face Lottie's mother and father. Maybe I should have given it more time. No, it is the right thing to do, coming here offering my sympathies. I ring the bell and wait. Her mother answers the door looking like she aged twenty years in these past few days.

'Anthony, do come in,' she says.

There is a smell of burned toast in the air.

She sniffs. 'Mrs Gibson, I'm… I…' I gave her the flowers. 'For you.'

She half smiles. 'Thank you. Would you like some tea?'

'No thanks.'

We sit in the rustic living room; there are photos above the fireplace, most of them of Lottie. The TV is on the BBC, but on mute. On the beige velvet sofa, there is a green throw-over. Mrs Gibson removes it and places it on the arm of the chair.

'The press are lurking about,' she announces, sinking into the chair.

'They are?' I ask, unable to mask my surprise.

'You didn't see them?'

'No, I haven't.'

'Maybe they left,' she says, taking out a tissue from her trousers. 'She had nothing but nice words to say about you. You made her happy, and for that, I'm grateful.'

She begins to sob. Nothing I say would bring back her daughter. No parent should bury their child, and Lottie was an only child. I peek at the photographs of Lottie on top of the fireplace. Lottie as a little girl on the beach standing by a sandcastle. Another of her with her parents as a teenager.

'Are there any updates?' I ask after she's calmed down.

She blows her nose, shaking her head. 'Did the police talk to you?'

I sit on the sofa. 'Yes, they did. Did they tell you how she...' I trailed off, unable to go on.

She dabs her eyes with the tissue. 'She was shot... Someone... shot her... in the face.'

If there was any colour in my face, it's gone now. My mouth gapes open. The words bounce around my head, *shot her in the face*. Her beautiful face, demolished, gone. My eyes grow moist. Who would do this to my friend? My lovely, sweet friend?

'They are going to interview everybody who had a connection with Lottie. Colleagues, friends, ex-boyfriends, anyone. She was so full of life, so optimistic.'

It occurs to me that Lottie's father is nowhere to be seen.

'Where is Mr Gibson?'

'He's in the garage. He hasn't come out since...'

I nod in understanding. 'Mrs Gibson.'

'Please call me Emily.'

'Emily, did Lottie tell you about a man? The police suspect she was seeing a man,' I pause, looking for the right word without upsetting her further, '...secretly.'

'A man?'

'The police asked me if... if there was another man besides Abdel... They believe she was seeing someone right after the break-up.'

Emily considers this. 'She didn't say. The police didn't tell us much...' She trails off as tears pour down her eyes. I give her time to recover.

'Is it okay if I go to her room?'

She wipes her nose. 'The police have already been there but yes, I suppose you can. It's upstairs to the left.'

'Thank you.'

She glances up at me as I rise. 'Why you want to see her room?'

'I just need... to get the feel of her. I miss her.'

She nods.

I have never been to her room, and it's as if I'm standing in a museum of a girl I once knew but now, she's not part of this world anymore, but of another. My chest tightens as I study the room. Her bedroom is a typical girl's room with flowery wallpaper, a single bed dressed with a white duvet and a stuffed toy in the middle. A stereo on the shelf with a collection of CDs, a few books and old magazines stacked neatly. On the dresser were jewellery boxes and photos with friends. I didn't know them. These photos were taken before I met her. Was she still in touch with these girls?

I cross the room and open the closet. A smell of fresh linen hits my nostrils. Dresses and jackets hang there, and on the bottom shelf are shoes, with bags on the top shelf.

I don't know what I'm looking for. Whatever was useful in this room, the police must have taken it. If she needed to hide something, she wouldn't hide it in here. I think of the password-protected file in her laptop. Whatever she was hiding, it's there and it haunts me. As I am about to close the closet, something attracts my attention. I squint at the photograph pinned on the door. It has a black background and neon colours that make the shape of a heart. This work is unfamiliar to me. It's professionally made, out of Photoshop or another advanced software. Where had she got this from? Did Abdel give it to her? How did the police miss this, or did they think it meant nothing to them? To me, it does.

I wrack my brain thinking of what Lottie liked that she could use as a password. I type her mother's name, her father's, Abdel's but no success. I even go as far as typing Davian's name and surname. Nothing. I cross out the places I visited on my map. I think about her apartment, but I can't go there; it's a crime scene.

****

Lottie's Recordings. Clip Four

I took my breaks outside with the view of the Thames and ate a packet of biscuits. It was lonely. All I did was file papers in that little room. I was so bored and I craved excitement. Anthony never came, nor Davian. When he did grace us with his presence, Davian glided past me with his nose up in the air, never looking down. He carried himself with a certain dignity and grace. A confident man.

After my break, I started towards the filing room. Davian stomped towards me looking like gold from a treasure chest. He had a set of papers in his hand while his musky rather oaky perfume slapped me across the face.

'Where have you been? I have been looking all over for you.' he demanded.

'I... was-'

'I don't care where you were, don't take off.'

'Um... uh, I didn't-'

'Don't waste my time. Here,' he said wryly, shoving a set of papers into my hands. 'Photocopy these for me, will you?'

'Okay,' I said.

Without another word, he marched off. A girl walked past him and stole a glance at the ice king. I didn't know where the photocopier was or how to use it. No one had shown me anything and I wasn't going to ask him; I feared he'd bite my head off. Lilia was behind her desk, typing.

'Lottie, how are you holding up?' she asked. She frowned when she saw my flustered expression.

'I uh... Davian asked me to do photocopies for him but I don't-'

She rolled her eyes. Is it because of me or the mention of Davian? 'Follow me.'

***

Davian is confrontational, and for someone like Lottie, he could come across as intimidating and hostile.

***

In the lift, Lilia pressed -1. I thought we were going to the parking area, but it was a large room with boxes; at the back, there was a large complicated-looking photocopier. Lilia explained to me how it worked.

'Remember what I showed you. I might not be here next time and if he asks you again, he won't help you.'

'Is he always like this?'

'He is used to having everything go his way. He can be difficult. You'll get used to him.'

She photocopied the papers and asked me to do the extra copies so I could get used to the machine.

'Would you like to go out for drinks?' she asked me.

My eyes widened; this woman wanted to go out for a drink with me?

'I would love that.'

'How about Friday night? We'll go after work?'

'Er... sure,' I said.

'Great, it's a date. Now go and hand him these before he gets all cross and moody.'

I realised I didn't know where his office was, so I had to ask the receptionist. I nearly crashed into him as he was on his way out.

'What took you so long?' he asked.

'I... I... didn't know-'

'You did them?' he asked.

'Yes.'

He snatched the photocopies from my hand, turned on his heel and shut the door on my face.

***

Lilia might know about this secret lover.

Chapter Eight

Sleeping was painful and waking up was painful. It hurt to go to sleep. It's all I can think about. I give my mom a call.

'Anthony, are you all right? I'm worried. I'm coming over,' she said.

'No, Mum, I'm fine, it's just I have lots on my mind.'

'I know you have a lot on your mind, but you weren't returning any of my calls. You said you'd call and if I don't hear from you, I worry.'

'I'm sorry, I didn't mean to worry you. I'll come around this afternoon, all right?'

***

Lottie's Recordings. Clip Five

Lilia and I went for cocktails afterwards. The filing room is starting to take shape. It will be finished in a week or so if Davian doesn't come around and stop me every five minutes. He comes and orders me about to get him this, get him that and photocopy this. The words thank you and please don't exist in his vocabulary. It's rude and frustrating. I tried to peek at his studio the other day, I couldn't make out much apart from a table with small photographs sorted in some order.

'Can I help you with something?' he asked.
'No-'

Before I could finish my sentence, I was greeted by the slam of the door.

How are Davian and Anthony best friends, again? They are nothing alike. At least Anthony is polite, warm, funny and friendly. Davian is cold, distant and he hardly ever smiles.

***

I thought with Lottie being my friend, Davian would go easy on her, but he didn't know her. She was a stranger to him and Davian is not the kind of person who is going to invite you to have lunch with him to get to know you. That's not how he functions; he only connects with people who are familiar to him and won't allow people in.

***

Lilia was beautifully turned out in an aquamarine pencil dress and nude pumps. I haven't invested in a new wardrobe yet; it will cost me a fortune to look like these people. Lilia asked me how Anthony and I became friends and I began to tell her. The waiter came over to our table and Davian walked in followed by a petite woman with short black hair. He smiled down at her, his eyes full of love and compassion. What I would give to have someone looking at me the way he looked at her. A power couple, I thought. I didn't know his girlfriend, but I couldn't help but feel a stab of jealousy. To sleep with him every night and wake up next to him. I want her life. Lilia followed where I was staring. His eyes drifted coldly at us. Lilia waved and the woman waved back, but Davian didn't and stomped to a free table. The woman followed him. What is it like to be with someone like him? Does he shut the door in her face too? I doubt it. He seems warm and gentle with her. The waiter came over with our drinks: mojito for me, Cosmopolitan for Lilia.

'You really like him, do you?' Lilia asked.

'Well, he's really handsome,' I gushed.

'And that was the woman who has him all to herself,' Lilia warned.

***

I had been rather sceptical about Lottie's fascination with Davian. I wondered why; he was rude to her, treated her as if she didn't exist and still it didn't stop her. Watching her talk about him is like listening to someone talking about their crush, but what if the innocent, harmless crush escalated into an obsession?

***

'Melissa is a talented photographer. She's the one who helped Davian to grow to what he is today and his photographs are pricey but they sell like hot cakes. Giselle worships him not only because he brings in the cash, but for his talent. Have you seen any of his work?' Lilia asked.

I shook my head.

Lilia took a sip from her cocktail. 'There are a few of his photographs in the gallery next door from the offices.'

'Well, I'm not big on art,' I said, playing with the straw.

She flipped her hair. 'You don't have to be a fan of art to appreciate the beauty of life. That's what his photographs are all about. Life and the people that pass through it... it resonates with many people.'

'How long have they been dating?' I asked.

'About three years, since he started working with Giselle. Melissa worked there longer but she travels back and forth between here and Japan and China.' Lilia leans closer and I do the same. 'Rumour has it,' she whispered, 'Melissa had a boyfriend when she met Davian and well, she was having something on the side with Davian and he convinced her to dump him and move in with him. They have been together ever since.'

As Lilia was pouring gossip, I noticed a man looking at me. He had brown skin, dark eyes and dreadlocks. He raised his glass and smiled. Lilia glanced back to see at who I was smiling at. Her mouth dropped and she clapped her hands together in excitement.

The man walked to our table. 'Ladies,' he said.

'Abdel!' Lilia squealed, getting up and putting her arms around him.

'And who is this beautiful girl?' he asked, looking at me.

***

It wasn't a rumour - it was true. Melissa had a boyfriend of two years until she started an affair with Davian and he managed to seduce her into leaving him.

Chapter Nine

My mum is a short plump woman with short dark hair. My parents live in Forest Hill. It's been nearly four years since I moved out. My mum comes out of the kitchen and gives me a hug.

'I'm so sorry. I know you loved her very much,' she says, squeezing me tighter.

'Thanks, Mum. Dad at work?' I ask.

She nods. 'Yes, would you like a cuppa?'

The house is silent apart from the ticking of the grandfather clock in the living room. The brown leather sofa still stands in the room with an old TV that Dad refuses to change. His record collection that I used to listen to as a kid is still stacked neatly. Nothing has changed. The house reeks of sadness and memories.

'I called Lottie's mum and offered my condolences. I'll send her flowers later on,' Mum says as we make it to the orange kitchen.

I see myself at five years old, where I used to play under the kitchen table. There are pieces of a jigsaw puzzle on it. Mum puts the kettle on, takes out a tin of biscuits and places it in front of me. I pick one and munch on it. She grabs two familiar mugs and places them on the counter.

'Are you eating?' she asks, gesturing at my skinny frame.

'Yes.'

To be honest, I haven't cooked a decent meal since the news had come out. All I have been eating is junk food, when I remember to eat. Mum would have a heart attack if I tell her this, so I lie so she won't worry.

'Oh, honey, I'm so sorry, you look so sad,' she says. 'Want to talk about it?'

'There isn't much to say...'

'Are you following the news?'

I shake my head. 'I'd rather not.'

'Two detectives came here the other day,' she said as the kettle started to boil.

The police were here at my mum's? Why? I swallow. 'Why?'

'To ask me questions about Lottie and you.'

'Me?' My heart thuds. 'What did they ask you about me?'

She takes out a carton of milk from the fridge. 'How long you knew her, how close you two were, about your childhood.'

My childhood? What had my childhood to do with Lottie's murder? I recall the ugly parts: my dad coming home from work, tired and grumpy. I was an energetic child, always playing and causing a racket in the house. Sometimes Dad lost his temper. Sometimes is an understatement; it happened often. He struck me once or twice. He's a big man over six feet tall. Mum used to get angry at him, so when he came home, she used to make me play in my room in order for my dad to have the peace and quiet he craved so much.

'Why didn't you call me?'

She places the mug in front of me. 'I did call you. You never pick up.'

'I have a lot on my mind,' I say, glancing down at my tea.

She takes a biscuit. 'It's good to talk.'

'I don't understand why someone would want to harm her.'

'Can you think of anyone?'

No, but Davian's name has come up more than once. No, Davian wouldn't do something like this. I know him; yes, he's cold and aloof, but not a killer.

'No,' I say.

'Maybe it's a stalker. You know how it is these days,' Mom says.

I consider this, Lottie becoming a victim of a lunatic. However, she knew the killer. Of this, I am sure. Those videos are a clue to who it might be.

***

Lottie's Recordings. Clip Six

I met Abdel for drinks last weekend. He's a photographer who does a few jobs for Giselle, but he mainly photographs models. We're taking it slow and I don't want to rush into a relationship. The other day, Davian told me from now onwards, any issues I might have, I pass them through him, not Giselle, as she has things to do. I don't like the tone he uses when speaking to me, with arrogance, superiority. Could this guy be any more overbearing?

***

Between her working there and seeing Abdel, I saw less of her and I had my own life. One time, I did go to the office to drop off a sculpture for Giselle. Lottie was sorting out the filing room which looked immaculate; she was proud of what she had done and I high-fived her for a job well done.

'I'm sorry we don't meet as often as we used to,' she said.

'It's okay, I'm busy too. How's Davian? Is he here?'

'I haven't seen him.'

'How are you holding up?' I asked her

She looked down at her shoes. 'It's okay.'

'Just okay?'

'Well, it's different.'

'Have you taken your break yet?'

'No.'

'Want to tell me all about it over a quick bite?'

She gave me a dazzling smile. 'I would love that.'

***

Davian enjoys wasting my time. As if I have nothing better to do. Like the other day, he sent me to buy him PE papers and other photographic equipment. He gave me a list of what he wanted.

I set off to find him the papers; it made me wonder why he doesn't go and buy them himself. I know nothing about photographic equipment. What if I get him the wrong thing and he tells me off? It cost me a full day of my work because I couldn't find the item anywhere in stock. I was about to give up when I found them in the last store. I returned with the items a little after six and he was putting on his coat.

'I don't need them now,' he said.

My blood boiled. Hot, angry tears curled into me. I opened his studio door and dumped the items on the floor.

***

I had no idea why he played those games with her; that's all they were, games. There were things she didn't tell me about, like this one. I suppose Lottie didn't tell me because she didn't want to create a strain between Davian and me.

I have to find out the places she had been to in the last three days of her life. She had dinner at the Japanese restaurant. No use for me to go there except to eat or to impress a lady. I need to speak to Ella again; I still need to talk to Abdel, Lilia and Davian.

Chapter Ten

I spent the rest of the night googling the murder. There are pictures of the police outside her apartment. *The Daily Mail* wrote the estimated time of death was around midnight. The neighbours heard nothing suspicious about that time apart from the music. No one saw anything out of the ordinary. A neighbour said she saw Lottie leaving the apartment 'all dolled up' at 7:30 pm.

I close the tab and I go to the password-protected folder again. I try her favourite city, Paris, and the dog she had until he died, Skittles. Nothing. I tapped my index finger on the keyboard. I log on to Facebook and go to her profile, which is filled with touching messages from her friends.

You are a flower, the moon and the stars. You were beautiful and always so full of life. Rest in peace, my dear friend and sister, Ella wrote.

I can't express the shock of this news. You were a wonderful friend, Lilia wrote.

I don't write anything; whatever I have to say, I'll say it to her at the funeral. I don't have to declare it to the world to show that I cared. I log out of Facebook and continue where I left off.

***

Lottie's Recordings. Clip Seven

This weekend, Abdel surprised me with a romantic trip to Venice; he went as far as calling Giselle and asking her if I could have the weekend off.

'That's not all,' he said.

'There is more?' I squealed.

'We're going to stay at The Gritti Palace,' he said, and began to tap on his tablet.

A few seconds later, he showed me pictures of the hotel as I covered my mouth with my hands in awe. 'It's beautiful; we'll be staying here?' I point at the screen.

He beamed proudly. 'Sure we are, babe.'

'I don't know what to say. I mean, no one's done anything like this for me before.'

He took my hand and rubbed it with his thumb. 'You deserve nothing but the best.'

I went back to work on Monday with a glow on my face. I walked past Davian. I held my head high as I wiggled past him; not even he was going to ruin my mood. Later that day, I was in the kitchen making myself a cup of coffee when Davian walked in.

'You are dating Abdel?' Davian asked, leaning against the door.

I wanted to tell him it's none of his business; it's not like he's told me anything about his life, why should I expose mine?

'How do you know?' I asked, pouring sugar in my coffee.

'I've seen you two together.' He helped himself to the fresh pot of coffee that I'd made.

Did he see us together? 'Where?'

He smirked. 'Does it matter?'

I blinked down at my coffee. Of course, he wasn't going to tell me. He leaned against the counter.

'You know he used to date Belle, the supermodel,' he said.

'Yes, I know.'

'At least, he makes you look desirable,' he snarled, before walking away.

I shut my eyes and tried to keep my breathing under control, but I couldn't. *He speaks to me as if I am dirt, he shuts the door in my face, he made me buy photographic equipment he didn't need just to amuse himself, but enough was enough. I will not be spoken to like this and keep my mouth shut. Yes, Abdel had a fling with a supermodel and yes, it makes me insecure. I mean, how can I even begin to compete with that? However, I reasoned Abdel was with me. He took me to Venice after all. I'm not a supermodel, but there had to be something about me he liked. Because Davian is good looking, it doesn't give him the right to walk all over me. I knew he thought Abdel made a downgrade compared to the likes of Belle, but Melissa was no movie star either. I slammed my hands so hard against the counter, the coffee splashed, making a round stain on the surface.*

'You're an arse!' I said through gritted teeth.

He turned. 'What did you say to me?'

'You heard me.' I said, walking into his personal space. 'You have no right to talk to me this way. I'm not here because I enjoy your dull company or anything like that. I'm here because I need the money.'

His stare was ice. Without saying a word, he left. That put him in his place.

The situation somehow got more uncomfortable. I had to do a bit of overtime, as I was behind on work. I was alone in the office. As I was about to enter the kitchen, a sniffing sound made me look over my shoulder; it sounded like someone had a cold and was blowing their nose.

It startled me because I'd thought I was alone. My eyes darted around, trying to detect where the sound had come from. I took another step forward then another and stopped when it came again. My throat tightened. It was coming from Davian's office. The door was open, which was odd; he never left the door open. I moved forward and glanced at the office. Davian was bent over his desk, there were photographs, and bottles of glues lined neatly one after another like soldiers. Alongside them were lines of white powder and a rolled-up bill. My mouth gaped open. I looked at the powder and at him. His face went red. It was so sad and pathetic. There he was, Giselle's star, abusing her trust. If she found out about this, Davian doing coke in her office, she'd have him fired. I scurried back, looking over my shoulder for a moment; I thought he'd come after me. He didn't. I went back to my desk, gathered my bag and I left through the fire exit to avoid running into him. I think he was too embarrassed to say anything, but I didn't want to take any chances.

***

It might have come as a shock to her, but Davian did coke and the reason wasn't to be social, or to party, nor to make him horny. He wasn't addicted to it. He took it to stay awake. Davian found sleep a waste of time and wanted to stay awake as much as possible. In order to do that, he had a supply of two things: coffee and coke.

***

I didn't tell anyone about it, but the urge was strong. I pictured it with grim satisfaction as I spread this to the office until it reached Giselle and she fired him. But I kept my mouth shut; it's not something you want to tell people about and Giselle wasn't going to take office gossip seriously. She would need proof. Davian didn't show his face in the office for three days.

I was on my way to do photocopies when he came out of Giselle's office. I kept my head low and went on, but he was behind me, strolling casually. My heart was in my mouth. I stopped and called for the lift. He stood beside me and said.

'Walk.'

My hands trembled. What he was going to do? What could he do? I descended the stairs with him behind me. I stood by the machine with my head bowed low, pressing the papers against my chest as if they would protect me. He stood in front of me.

'Look at me, Lottie,' he said in a low soothing voice.

I looked at him and swallowed.

'Did you tell anyone?' he asked in the same calm voice.

It was as if my mouth was made of cloth and it was suffocating me. I shook my head.

'Are you sure?' he asked.

I nodded.

'Even if you talked, no one would believe you. It's your word against mine and who do you think they are going to believe: me or the help?'

I dropped my hands to my sides, clutching them into fists. The nerve of this guy. The little shit.

'Do you think you are so important that I would go around and talk about you? I didn't even know you were there and I don't care,' I snapped, turning my back to him and getting on with my work. 'You're the one who cares since you felt the need to bring it up. Now, if you'll excuse me, Giselle needs these ASAP.'

I stabbed buttons on the photocopier, but I felt his hot stare on my back.

'Fine...' he said.

***

What was he thinking anyway? What if Giselle walked in? He'd be out of a job in no time. The one thing Giselle hates is people taking advantage of her. Lottie did keep her word; she didn't even mention this to me.

***

This morning, I met Lilia for breakfast before work. After we ordered our coffees and scrambled eggs on toast, she leaned closer and placed her hand on mine.

'What?' I said.

'I don't want to alarm you, but I have some bad news,' she said, pouting her lips.

'What's wrong?' I said.

'Last night, Taylor had her speaker on and she heard Giselle and Davian talking.'

'What about?'

She pointed her finger at me.

I pointed at myself. 'Me?'

I knew what it was about, and Davian was going to make it impossible for me to be left in peace, not after what I had seen.

'He told her you don't fit in and to have you,' she made bunny ears with her fingers, 'removed.'

'Why?' I cried.

She fell silent as the waiter placed two plates of scrambled eggs and toast in front of us, along with two steaming cups of coffee. Lilia reached for the ketchup, and the bottle made farting sounds when she squeezed it.

'Apparently Giselle asked him the same thing; why do you want me to have her removed? Did she insult a client? Have you caught her stealing? I can't fire a girl because you think she doesn't fit in,' Lilia said.

I buried my face in my hands. It was about what I saw, it had to be. I'd told him I wouldn't tell anyone and I had no intentions of doing so.

'He really hates me,' I cried.

Lilia regarded me. 'He's a prick. Let me have a word with him.'

'No, no, I already did.'

Lilia stared at me. 'You did? When was this?'

I told her what he'd said to me in the kitchen. Lilia laughed until she was in tears.

'You really called him an arse? You go, girl.'

'Is Giselle going to fire me?'

Lilia shrugged. 'I wouldn't worry about it if I were you, she's not going to fire you unless there is a legit reason. Ignore him, he'll get over it. Now eat up. You'll need your strength.'

***

Lottie showed up at my door unexpectedly when this happened, but I didn't know the truth behind it until now. She brought an Indian take-out and a bottle of wine.

'Davian hates me,' she announced over dinner.

'Uh, what makes you think that?' I asked, picking up a forkful of the chicken curry.

She cut the naan bread in tiny pieces. 'He wants me gone.'

'Gone?'

'From work. He doesn't like me.'

'So? He's not your boss, tell him to bugger off.'

'I did, but he went to Giselle and demanded she should have me "removed" because I don't fit in. I didn't think he'd do something like this.'

'I'll have a word with him,' I said.

'No, please. I don't want to look like I came crying to you, and I can speak for myself.'

'Yeah, you did and it didn't work. I'll have a word with him.'

I went to the flat that Davian shares with Melissa. A tiny one-bedroom apartment, a perfect room for damaged goods, as he likes to describe himself. When I got there, the flat was pitch black, apart from a lamp on his desk. I visualised the apartment, the fitted carpets on the floors, and white painted walls. There was photographic equipment on the wall unit, vinyls and books stacked on a bookshelf. The apartment was like their little solitary confinement. Two lovers stuck in their artistic world in their own personal space.

'How do you work like this?' I asked him through the gloom.

'Would you like anything to drink?' he offered, ignoring my comment.

'I'm fine.'

He lit a cigarette. I did the same.

'I don't know what you're playing at. First, I thought it's your way to amuse yourself, but it's not funny, anymore,' I said.

He looked at me dumbstruck. 'What are you talking about?'

'The stunt you pulled with Giselle? Come on, mate, Lottie is upset. Apologise to her and leave her alone. She's a nice girl.'

'I know she's a nice girl,' he said, exhaling smoke into the air.

'Then be nice to her. Why are you tormenting her? Is it because she's my friend?'

Davian arched his eyebrows. 'What the hell is that supposed to mean?'

'You know exactly what it means, Davian.'

He gave me a hard look. 'Are you in love with her?'

'What?'

'You heard me.'

'She's my friend.'

He kept looking at me sharply. 'That's not what I asked.'

'I care for her,' I said, glaring at him.

He shrugged. 'Fine. I'll apologise.'

'Davian!'

'I will, I'll promise.'

Chapter Eleven

Abdel lives somewhere in Greenwich, but I'm not sure exactly where. We aren't close; I would call him an acquaintance. I've run to him at events and with Lottie, although when she and I met, it was the two of us. The times we spent together were uninterrupted by those around us. If anyone walked by and looked at us, they would have thought we were brother and sister.

I don't know what I can get out of him since they broke up six months ago. After she ended their relationship, I obviously asked her why.

'Life,' she said.

Now that I think about it, she might have dumped him because there was someone else involved. This mystery man, her killer. I call Ella.

'Why do you want to track him down?' she asks.

I make out noises in the background, ambient music and voices.

'Just to see how he is,' I say.

I don't want anyone to know I have Lottie's laptop in my possession. I can't trust anyone; what's to stop them from telling the police? If I tell Ella, she will try to convince me to do the right thing. I will hand it over, in time, when I'm done, although I have to find a way to do it. I can't waltz into the police station with the computer of a dead girl.

Abdel's apartment is a clutter of cameras piled on the coffee table. There are photographs on the floor. A pizza box and an empty bottle of vodka, along with cans of soft drinks on the sofa. There are crumbs on the carpet and a hint of cigarettes and mould in the air. The curtains are shut which makes the living room murky. His eyes are red and puffy; these past few days haven't been good to him either.

'It's a nightmare,' he says. 'I can't believe it, I mean, why?'

'I don't know.'

He sighs. 'Can I get you anything? I'm afraid I don't have much.'

'I'm good.'

He takes a bottle of vodka from the cabinet and unscrews the top. 'That night, I had dinner with my family. My nephew, he turned eighteen, so we all went out. I stayed there till about one and went home to sleep.'

'Abdel,' I said.

He takes a swing of vodka. 'What?'

I take out the photograph, the one I took from Lottie's closet, from my coat pocket, and hold it out to him so he can have a clear look.

'What is that?' he asks.

'Take a closer look,' I say.

He squints at the photo and curls his lips. 'I never saw that before.'

'It's an abstract photograph. I found it in her closet.'

He stares at me. 'I know what it is, but I never saw it before.'

I put the photo back in my pocket. 'I'm wondering where she got it from. I figured you might have given it to her.'

'I didn't.'

'Okay.'

He sits on the sofa. 'You two were so close, I could never have that with her; she didn't look at me the way she looked at you.'

I don't have time to listen to this.

'Did you two…?'

'No need to torture yourself or me with this. I lost my best friend.'

'And I lost a woman who I used to date,' he says.

His voice is sharp enough to cut through steel.

'Fair enough,' I say.

I sit across from him. I remove the plastic Pepsi bottle from under my arse and place it on top of the pile on the coffee table.

'When she broke it off, what did she did say exactly?' I ask.

'She didn't give me a reason. I swear she didn't. She only said it's over and she didn't want to do this anymore. I pleaded with her to give me a reason. I needed closure, at least, so I could move on peacefully. I kept wondering what I could have done wrong.' His eyes dart to me. 'I wondered if it was because of him she ended it, at first. I thought it was because of you.'

I lean forward. 'Wait, you think she dumped you for who?'

'Davian, who else?' he says

That's preposterous. Davian is no saint, but I find it hard to believe.

'Why on earth she would dump you for Davian?' I ask.

'Well,' Abdel says, and pauses to take a gulp from the vodka, 'she passed comments about his looks.'

'Because she made comments about Davian's looks it doesn't mean she was sleeping with him,' I reason.

'I don't know, it's weird.'

I raise my eyebrow. 'What's so weird?'

His eyes narrow. 'Her relationship with him.'

'They were work colleagues, not even friends. They didn't have a relationship. All the guy did was give her a hard time.'

He rubs his chin. 'Did he though?'

'What are you talking about?'

'Okay,' he says, planting his legs wide. 'I go to surprise her at work, right? I thought it would be nice, you know, she was my girl. I looked for her in her cubical and she wasn't there. It was late. No one was in the office. I went down to the photocopy room. I figured she might be there. I knew my way around the place since I did work for Giselle before. The door was open and I saw them.'

Abdel looks ahead as if he's remembering the whole thing. 'They were by the photocopier, him and Lottie. They were talking. I heard her giggle, he took his phone out, and he saw me and said something to her, maybe that I was watching. She looked at me and left the room her face flushed. She seemed nervous, reeking of tension, as if she had been caught. She kept touching her ear and adjusting her skirt. When I asked what was that all about, she said that Davian was giving her instructions regarding an upcoming exhibition.'

'Did you believe her?'

'I wanted to, but if he was simply giving her instruction, why the flushed cheeks? The nervousness? The adjusting of clothes?'

'You think they had sex?'

'I don't know,' he says.

We fall silent and he starts to roll a joint with shaking hands. 'It was weird. I knew she had a crush on him, no doubt about that. The thing is she didn't try to hide it, not even from me. I suspected Davian knew it too. I mean the guy is no fool but secretly, he liked her too, at least that's what I think.'

'You think so?'

'I know what I saw in that room. It had nothing to do with two people not getting along. Maybe there was something going on, and all of that was an act so no one would suspect.'

'Do you remember when you saw them in the copy room?' I ask.

He lights the joint and takes a puff, tilting his head back. 'Not the date exactly, but a few weeks before the party.'

A few weeks before the party, now that I recall, she stopped complaining. I'd thought Davian might have apologised to her after all. I need a calendar to follow the timeline. Abdel offers me the joint and I take a few puffs. I can't get high. I have to go back to my place and figure out what was going on between her and Davian.

Chapter Twelve

The event happened in March of last year. I go through the calendar on my phone. I scroll to the date. Davian claimed he had no relationship with Lottie outside the office, just a colleague, but it seems to be more than that. How could he stand there and lie to my face! Abdel had brought a new perspective I hadn't considered before.

The party was on Friday, I had an exhibition the Saturday after, and the party was the previous week. Abdel said he saw Davian and Lottie a few weeks before in the copy room. Davian might have planned to break them up. Why? It makes sense why he said those things to Abdel, but he had Melissa to consider? He wouldn't tell Abdel those things about Lottie and me in an innocent way - it was intentional. Davian admitted he couldn't see the error of his ways. The question is, what happened in the period when Abdel broke up Lottie? Is Davian the other man?

***

Lottie's Recordings. Clip Eight

When I returned to work on Monday, I saw Davian. He glared my way. He was in one of his moods again, so I armoured myself for what was to come. I went to hide in my cubical. My desk was piled with documents for filing and I went on with my work right away. Afterwards, I returned to my cubical and scowled at my desk; there was a photo that I'm sure wasn't there before. It had a black background with colourful images in the shape of a large heart.

***

I pause the video and take out the photo from my coat pocket and examine it. She is referring to the same photo. Black background and colourful images that come in the shape of a heart. It has to be it. Tell me, Lottie, did Davian give it to you?

***

There was no message. I kept the photo on my desk and didn't think about it for the rest of the day.

During lunch, I went to get a sandwich with Lilia and asked her if she'd put a photograph on my desk.

'Me? Why would I do that?' she asked.

'I don't know, you tell me.'

I opened my chicken sandwich and a packet of crisps.

'Was it there before you cleared your desk?' she asked, tucking into her salad.

'Nope.'

'Maybe Giselle put it there.'

'Without saying anything? It's unlike her.'

Lilia shook her head. 'Yeah, it's not like her.'

We ate in silence.

'Where is it?' she asked me, pouring water into her glass.

I chewed on my sandwich. *'On my desk.'*

'Show it to me when we get back.'

'Okay.'

Lilia inspected the photo carefully when I showed it to her. She handed it back to me, her face blank.

'So?' I asked.

'Maybe Abdel placed it there.'

'Without saying anything? Why would he come here anyway?'

'I don't know. Ask him.'

In the evening, I met Abdel. We stopped to get pizza on the way to my place.

'Did you come to the office today?' I asked, taking a slice of pizza from the box.

'No, I didn't, why?' he asked.

'No reason.'

In the gallery were lines of photographs. I surveyed each photo, not knowing what I was looking for. The photos were of people mostly: an old man, children playing in the park, and a landscape. I moved to a beautiful collaged image of Japan, judging by the oriental building. There was nothing abstract.

'What are you doing down here?'

Davian was by the door dressed in a checked shirt and black trousers.

'I'm... er... nothing.'

'Nothing?' he asked.

I cleared my throat and tried again. 'I'm looking for something.'

'What are you looking for?'

'A meaning.'

'Of what?'

His footsteps echoed on the marble floor. 'What? I don't have all day, Lottie,' he snapped.

I took a deep breath. Funky house music played in the background. The office had the same music playing, as if someone would stop what they were doing and start to dance.

He snatched the photo from my hand and studied it.

I took my time to study him. Melissa could hold him and glance into those eyes. I never saw much of her nor spoke to her, and I had nothing to say to her. Still, I envied her. Davian handed me the photo.

'So?' I asked.

'It's mine.'

'You put it on my desk?'

'I did.'

'Why?' I cried.

'Do I need a reason to give you something?' he said, flashing me a smile so dazzling, I felt was being sucked into him.

***

I grabbed the photo and looked at it. Davian gave her this photo? What was it doing in her old bedroom?

***

'Let's start over, okay?' he said.

'What am I going to do with this?' I asked foolishly.

'I don't know, frame it. Is that why you're down here? Hoping you'll find something similar?'

'Er... yes.'

'You won't find it, not here, not anywhere.'

'No?'

His eyes searched my face. I think for the first time, he actually saw me. He smiled again. This change in his attitude took me by surprise. For how long will it last?

'Because it's one of a kind.'

Was this his way of saying I'm one of a kind? Something inside me twitched. A picture is worth a thousand words. Isn't that what they say?

'One of a kind,' I repeated.

'Yeah, everyone is,' he said and walked past me.

Leaving me there cold and empty. For that moment, for that instant, I thought... I don't know what I thought.

Chapter Thirteen

A computer, a piece of machinery, has invaded my life, but I can't let it go. The need to find out what happened is my focus. This is what I have left, a laptop where Lottie resurrects to tell me what she had been through. Why had she given me this laptop, knowing what it contained? It haunts me. Did she know she was going to die? Is that why she gave it to me? Hoping I'd see those video clips in time? If she was in danger, why didn't she say anything? Why not go to the police?

***

Lottie's Recordings. Clip Nine

Anthony and I met for a drink. He told me he's seeing someone: a girl called Oli. I don't see much of him. I miss his company and I don't think Oli likes that we meet alone.

***

I was in an exhibition when I saw a beautiful girl dressed in a black dress striding by, flicking her long black hair. I watched her for a while before building up the courage to approach her. She was admiring one of my sculptures. I walked over to her and asked her if she knew the artist. Oli had a round face with high cheekbones, full lips and cornflour blue eyes. She told me she was studying art and was doing a project on sculptures. It was love at first sight, for me at least. It would have lasted longer if Davian hadn't swept in and shit all over it with his big mouth. Lottie got it all wrong; Oli didn't mind me meeting her alone. We're adults, not kids.

***

'How is Abdel?' Anthony asked when we sat across from each other in a lounge bar.

'Good, he's doing a shoot in Paris,' I said. 'How is Oli?'

'Studying.'

I picked up the menu. 'Shouldn't you be helping her?'

'If she needed my help, she'd ask for it.'

'Uhhh... Mr Sharp.'

'I offered. She said she's fine.'

I close the menu. 'I miss us.'

He glanced at me. 'Whatever happens, we will always be friends,' he said, reaching out for my hand.

I took his hand. 'No, that's not what I meant.'

I wanted him to understand: I missed how we used to be, where we could meet up regularly. It was my way to tell him I love him. A figure approached our table.

***

Davian happened to be in the same bar accompanied by Melissa who was in town; this was the first time she and Lottie were introduced. Lottie kept staring up at Davian until Melissa appeared behind him and Lottie turned her focus to her. Studying the competition, I think.

***

Anthony stood to greet him and Melissa. I didn't stand up. I was curious to look at the woman who'd conquered Davian's cold heart.

She was pretty, with sleek black hair cut in a bob, flawless complexion and dark eyes.

'Lottie,' he said.

'Davian.'

'Melissa, my girlfriend,' he said.

He sounded such a douche when he said girlfriend, as if I wasn't aware and needed to be reminded. It was a silent message on his part; I know you like me, but I can never be yours, never have been, and never will be. I shook her hand. It was freezing cold. She smiled at me. Anthony watched me closely, as if I was about to do something dangerous.

'So, what you guys up to?' Anthony asked Davian.

'We just came in this,' he gestured at the bar with its wooden table and chairs and vintage pictures on the grey walls, 'glamourous establishment for a drink.'

His voice reeked with sarcasm.

'You work with us, correct?' Melissa said to me. *'I've seen you about, but we never had time to be properly introduced.'*

'Yes, I do,' I said, giving Anthony a sideways glance.

'Of course, I spend most of the time hopping on and off planes,' she went on.

Unlike Davian, she seemed more approachable and warmer, but then again, we were keeping up appearances here. It's not like we would become best friends.

'Why don't you join us?' Anthony said.

I hated him for inviting them. I thought we were supposed to catch up.

Davian hesitated. *'What do you think?'* he asked Melissa.

'I would love to,' she said.

Anthony moved beside me so Melissa and Davian could sit beside each other. I ordered another glass of red wine from the waiter. From under the table, I found Anthony's hand and grabbed it.

Davian and Melissa ordered a bottle of Perrier and two glasses of wine. Davian was a mystery. A novelty, and I didn't know anything about him. Anthony hardly talked about him. It was strange. Their whole friendship was strange to me. All I know about him is that he's my age and a respected photographer. That night, I learned he didn't like to drink, ate very little, Perrier is his water of choice, and he's the middle child; he had a sister two years older than him and a brother a *year younger than him. His brother is also involved in the art world but didn't do any work for Giselle.*

***

What was it with her and Davian, anyway? It annoyed me, the fixation she had grown over him. Davian wasn't accessible to her, but he became a curiosity.

Chapter Fourteen

I'm wondering if Lottie played us all for fools and led us to believe she was innocent as a prom queen, but in reality, she wasn't. I'm about to discover everything and I didn't know what to do with this explosive secret. The question is killing me: why she lent me her laptop knowing what it contains. Why Lottie? What was Lottie going through that she couldn't tell me in person? Have I failed her? What if I never knew her at all and there is more to her than I was led to believe?

Lilia is sitting by the window when I walk into the café. I approach her table; Lilia greets me with a hug

Lilia takes my hand. 'How can I help?'

'Lottie was seeing someone in secret. Did she ever mention or make any indication that she was... you know... seeing someone in secret?'

Lilia lifts the coffee cup to her lips. 'If the police are suspecting that Lottie was seeing someone, they must have evidence to support it, right?' She pauses. 'I'm going to tell you what I have told the police.' She pauses again, for effect this time. 'I suspected there might have been someone.'

A waitress comes to take my order and after she leaves, Lilia looks at me wide eyed.

'Lottie wouldn't tell me,' she continues, 'I don't know why she didn't. I mean we were friends. I respected her wishes; if she didn't want to tell me, fine, but if she told me, I could have helped her more.'

I raise an eyebrow. 'What do you mean help her?'

'I told the police,' she says, looking across the room as if someone can overhear our conversation, 'everyone has secrets, you and I. Something we are ashamed of, a past, or something we've done something we don't want anyone to find out about. It's what makes us human after all, but with her, not only did she have secrets, which was fine by me, but she was sneaky.'

My shoulders go tight. 'Sneaky?'

'Yeah, I think she was fooling around with a married man; if he wasn't married, he must have been in a relationship.'

The waitress arrived with my tea and a chicken salad for Lilia.

I reach for the milk and pour three sugars in my tea. 'How did you find this out?'

Lilia lifts her fork and tosses her salad with it. 'She wasn't secretive before, but she changed. It was sudden... unexpected.'

'When was this?' I ask, stirring my tea, 'I mean... was this when she was with Abdel or after?'

'After,' she pauses, thinking. 'Yes, after she broke up with him.'

The tea was still hot. 'So, it was after the party?'

'Yes.'

I lean closer and she does the same. 'Do you think it's Davian, the man she was fooling around with?'

She wrinkles her nose and lowers her voice. 'You think she and Davian were having an affair?'

I lean back on my seat. 'That is what I'm beginning to suspect.'

'Did you confront him?'

'No, not yet, but he gave her a photograph.'

Lilia presses her lips together. 'A photograph?'

I'm about to tell her, yes, she told you about it, but then Lilia will wonder how I know Lottie showed it to her. So, I explained the design to her.

'Lottie did show me a photo similar to what you're referring to. Someone left it on her desk. So, it was him who gave it to her? She never mentioned it again. He gave her a photo, but it doesn't prove they were having sex.'

'No, but... it's weird. After the party, everything changed. She changed,' I say.

That's where I need to go: to the party, when it all started, where everything came crumbling down for her and me.

'Well, she was into him. There are girls in the office who are in love with him... you know, a harmless office crush, but hers... I don't know. It's like he was an obsession.'

Lilia takes a sip from her coffee. 'Whatever it was, she was out of her depth, and she got too sucked into it.'

'What did she get sucked into?'

'Whatever she had been doing...' She placed the fork down and pushed the chair forward, so close to the table, that there was no space for her to move.

'One time, a few weeks after she broke up with Abdel, I found her crying in the bathroom. She was a mess; she had been crying so much, I didn't know what to do to calm her down. She was shaking and could hardly breathe from sobbing, hiccupping, that sort of thing.'

The waitress comes over to serve me my sandwich. I leave it in front of me.

'And?'

Lilia pushes the plate aside. 'I couldn't make out what she was saying. I told her, Lottie I can't hear you, stop crying, calm down. Lottie bit into the toilet paper, tearing it with her teeth, she was in so much pain. I thought someone close to her had died, or because of Abdel at the time, that she regretted it. She kept saying, 'oh what am I thinking, I can't have it, it's all a lie, an illusion. I'm a fantasist, I was so wrapped up in my bubble that I failed to see the signs. Now, my bubble is burst and I don't know what to do.' What, Lottie? What happened? I asked her. Lottie wouldn't tell me; she kept staring at the tiles. She was hysterical, grabbing her hair as if she wanted to tear it out of her scalp. Lottie said through gritted teeth, 'I'll find a way, I will not be played, I know a way. I fucked up my life to make a total fool of myself.' I couldn't possibly understand what she was going through and if she'd told me, I would have helped. I tried to get it out of her but no use, she wouldn't budge. I wondered, who would do this to her? Those words were aimed at someone, the person who had caused her this pain. I said to her, what are you talking about? Tell me what's wrong, I can help you. 'No one can help me, but I'll hit where it hurts', she said.'

'Hit where it hurts,' I repeated.

Lottie, what did you do?

Lilia pushes the chair back, allowing the space. 'Yes, I didn't realise it then, but it was about a guy.'

I pick up my sandwich and take a bite. The cheddar explodes in my mouth.

I eat quietly while Lilia looks out the window.

'The strangest thing was, the next day, she was as happy as a clam. It was as if what I witnessed wasn't real,' Lilia said, looking at a group of girls a few tables away.

The sandwich starts to grow in my mouth.

Lilia returns her gaze to me. 'Did you two have a row or something to make her behave so oddly?'

'No. We hardly ever argued,' I say.

Apart from the night of the party. It was a messed up, confusing night I'd rather not think about. Was it because of me? Did I get her that upset? I play with my teaspoon. She told Lilia she'd fucked up her life to make a total fool of herself, and this was a few weeks after she broke up with Abdel. It could be aimed at me. I tap the teaspoon on the cup; no, it had to be someone else, someone who promised her something but didn't deliver. At least she thought of it that way.

Chapter Fifteen

I drop on the sofa exhausted. After Lottie had dinner with Ella, she went back to her apartment to meet him, this man, this lover, and her killer. Was Davian involved? Was he the man she was seeing in secret? The prospect of them together seems ridiculous, but not farfetched. But he had Melissa to consider... why would he cheat on her?

Lottie's Recordings. Clip Ten

I don't know what's up with Abdel. He has been acting strange lately. It's been like this since he came to surprise me at work and saw Davian and I talking in the copy room.

I was unaware Davian was still in the building. He stood by the door silent as a ghost.

'Would you like some tea?' he asked, handing me a plain porcelain mug from the kitchen.

'Thank you,' I said, shutting the copier and placing the mug on top of it.

'Are you attracted to me?' he asked.

I desperately thought of how to answer. The question was forward, coming from someone like Davian, who hardly ever asked personal questions or allowed any form of friendship. He was locked away in his little world and only a few people were allowed in there. I longed to be one of those people.

'What makes you think that?' I asked.

'Isn't it obvious?'

'If it's so obvious, why are you asking me? To hear me say it aloud?'

'No, but I noticed how you look at me, how you don't look at me.'

'Even if I'm attracted to you, I would never act on it,' I said.

He waited.

'I can't explain it,' I said. 'I don't understand it.'

'Do you want to understand it?' he asked.

Where was he going with this. He kept on waiting while I struggled to find the right words. Was he trying to tempt me?

'I have a boyfriend and you have… Melissa.'

'That's one of the reasons it would never happen.'

How many reasons did he have? So he'd thought about it?

'And I like older women… I like intelligent conversations,' he went on.

I didn't know what to say. He was about to turn to leave then changed his mind, rubbing his jaw.

'I'm struggling,' he said.

'With what?'

'I don't know why people find… me… good looking. I'm rather clumsy.'

Why was he telling me this? It puzzled me for days. He's supposed to say this to Melissa. I thought, here is a man who has no idea how handsome he truly is, failing to see what people see. How women swooned over him. I liked the modesty of it. I wanted to stroke his cheek and run my hand through his hair. Davian's phone beeped. He took it out from his pocket and muttered.

'The groom is here.'

Abdel stood there with a look as if he'd seen a ghost. I went to him. Davian strolled towards us.

'Abdel,' he said

'Davian,' Abdel said.

When he was gone, Abdel asked, 'What was that all about? I thought you two didn't get on?'

'We don't, he was just giving me instructions.'

That was the first time I lied to Abdel.

I spent the remaining week running errands for Giselle. She's going to host a party as the company is celebrating its seventh anniversary. She does this every year, where she invites her friends, staff and elite clients. I went to the printers to print out the invitations. I went to the post office, to send out those invitations to her clients. Giselle didn't believe in running an event on Facebook to save time. When I suggested this, she looked at me as if I'd said the stupidest thing. I picked up the tablecloths from the dry cleaners, made sure the flowers, the drinks and food were in order. I enjoyed this; it kept me busy and it was different from the dull tasks usually given to me. After the incident in the copy room, I hardly saw Davian. I liked that he opened a bit of himself to me. Sometimes, I saw Melissa go in his studio and not come out or I'd miss her coming out. I wonder what they do in there. Have sex I presume.

A week after the party, there will be an exhibition where Davian's new set of photographs are going to be displayed. I had been assigned to assist. I can't wait to see them.

The party was on Friday and partners were invited. Anthony was going to be there and I couldn't wait to see him. The last time I'd seen him was when we went for a drink and Davian had crashed it. Since it was a formal event, and I had nothing to wear for it, I went out, bought a new outfit and blew my entire budget! The choice of dress was something a sales assistant picked out for me. A sheer black top that I had to wear a boob tube underneath and a blue pleated skirt and gold high-heeled sandals.

***

I remember her as if it was yesterday. I'd never seen her like that, all dressed up looking like a princess. It was a chance for Lottie to leave an impression and she was going to make the most of it.

Chapter Sixteen

I cook steak and chips for dinner, the first decent meal I've had in days. I sit in front of the laptop and proceed with the next video. Unlike the others, her face is not showing, as if she were ashamed; her voice is hoarse as if she had been crying when this was filmed.

***

Lottie's Recordings. Clip Eleven

Abdel looked handsome in an all-black suit. I held his hand and told him I loved him and he shrugged it off as if it meant nothing. He didn't seem to believe me. What did he see in that copy room that freaked him out so much? I was only talking to a co-worker. He seemed to drift further apart from me. Does he doubt me? Does he think I'm cheating?

***

It wasn't just any co-worker, Lottie, it was Davian. I think Abdel was put off by the whole situation with Davian. It started to bother him. If Davian had locked the door in the copy room and seduced her, would she give in or stop him? I feel sorry for Abdel having to compete with someone that, in her eyes, he would never match up to.

***

Abdel stopped to talk to some people.

'This is my friend Lottie,' he said.

I gave him a sideways glance. We had been sleeping with each other for month; how am I a friend, exactly? I stomp to the bar and get myself a drink. Giselle walked in looking a million dollars in a long black evening gown accompanied by a gorgeous tall black man. His skin was dark brown, he had chocolate, velvety eyes, his hair was shaven, and he looked like he spent a lot of time in the gym. Was he her husband? Abdel came by my side, putting a hand round my waist, and planted a kiss on my cheek. I smiled, pushing the friend thing away. A few people moved away and Anthony appeared. Oli was with him. Davian entered alone, no Melissa on his arm. He looked elegant in a leather blazer. When he waltzed in, for a second, I thought the crowd was going to move aside so he could pass; he had that presence. He stopped beside Anthony and they greeted each other. For friends who'd known each other since childhood, something seemed off. There was that frosty aura between them. Davian looked me up and down.

'Lottie, you look beautiful,' Davian said.

I went pink. 'Oh... thank you.'

***

In Lottie's eyes, she might have thought Davian and I were cold with each other, but we weren't. No one could forget the glare Abdel had passed at her as she stood there turning from pink to red. Abdel looked like a man who wanted to be anywhere but there. His eyes kept darting around the room, looking uncomfortable, if not embarrassed, sipping on his drink, nodding and talking only when a question needed a response.

***

Anthony and I left Abdel, Oli and Davian to chat while we went to the bar to get drinks.

'He introduced me as a friend,' I said to Anthony.

Anthony gave me a look which said, 'this isn't the time or place', but he listened.

'A friend? Can you believe it?' I went on.

'I'm sure he didn't mean it that way, or maybe they weren't close enough to introduce you as his girlfriend,' he said.

'Bollocks,' I said.

Melissa walked in, dressed in a sophisticated black suit and went straight to Davian. God, I envied her. I watched how she looked at him, how he looked at her. I studied them as if they were two wild animals on the Discovery Channel. I took a sip of champagne; the bubbles danced and glided into my mouth, tasting like happiness. I want that, I thought to myself: a man who would look at me that way. I watched how he pulled her close and kissed her on the cheek, while her face lit up as if she'd won the lottery. Despite his cold, unapproachable exterior, he kept her happy, seemed like a good boyfriend. Maybe the long-distance thing does work. She looked up at him and smiled, then playfully hit his shoulder. When he smiled, it seemed as if the world would light up. She whispered something in his ear, her hand touched his, and he glanced at her and laughed. Let's face it, I'm just an assistant with no ambitions. Nothing motivates me, I have no talent - just a silly girl. I'm not a catch, while Melissa, as beautiful as she is, is also talented and has a career of her own. She is the full package. Why am I comparing myself to her?

***

Did she think this was a competition? As much she couldn't stand it, Davian was with Melissa and there was nothing Lottie could do about it. I'm coming to the part of those clips that I am not going to like. Was she planning to do something stupid like seduce him? It had to be, how she described the whole thing as if she were a predator studying its prey. All of this was happening under my nose, and I didn't even notice how she was looking at them? Well, looking is not a crime, if only I'd taken a second. That was all I needed, a second, I would have noticed she was up to something. If I had, she might still be alive.

***

At some point during their flirtation, Davian looked straight at me. I sighed and I laid my head on Anthony's shoulder. He gazed down at me. I looked at his lips. If it wasn't for the room full of people, I would have kissed him.

***

There it was, the gesture that made Abdel and Oli question our friendship. I knew she wanted to kiss me and I backed away. It was too late; we had been seen. I felt betrayed by Lottie. She was using me to make Abdel jealous and I hate those games. I didn't want to be part of her vendetta against her boyfriend. I had a good relationship with Oli and I wasn't going to let it dissolve because of a misunderstanding. If Lottie had issues with Abdel, she should have addressed them to him.

'Seriously, Lottie,' I told her.

I moved away from her. Oli was waiting for me, and her jaw was set.

'What the hell?' Oli asked. 'She should have fucked you on the dance floor. That girl is trouble.'

'She's a little drunk. Don't take any notice of her.'

'Don't give me that crap,' Oli said, raising her voice a little and a few guests scowled at us. 'I heard Davian talking to Abdel.'

'What?'

'I've heard everything. He told him Lottie wants you for her own. Your own best friend said that.'

I wanted to kill him with my bare hands. Davian doesn't think before he speaks. Oli walked away and I chased after her.

***

I found Abdel outside smoking a cigarette. I placed my hand over his shoulder, but he brushed it away.

'What's going on?' he demanded. 'What is going on between you and him? I know what I saw in there.' Abdel took a long drag of his cigarette, 'You're sleeping with him, aren't you?'

My heart jumped out of my chest. 'Anthony and I are friends. What I did was silly, but-'

'Silly? You're into him! Am I supposed to believe you knew him all of those years and the thought never crossed your mind?'

I placed my hand over my chest. 'No, never.'

He shook his head in disbelief.

'What did Davian say to you?' I asked.

'That you two are more than just friends.'

My hands clenched into fists. 'That son of a bitch!'

'I don't want you to talk to him anymore,' Abdel said, crushing the cigarette under his heel.

My heart began to pound loud now. Stop talking to Anthony? That is not happening.

'But he's my friend, I'm not going to give him up'

He pointed his finger. 'You are not willing to give up a friend for me?'

I took a step closer as if to challenge him. 'No, I'm not. How would you feel if I asked you to give up a friend of yours?'

'It's clear we are not in the same place. At least quit that job.'

'What?' I raised my voice now.

'Quit. I don't want you to work there anymore.'

Heat rushed through me. 'You want me to stop talking to Anthony and quit my job. What do I do then?'

Abdel's face softened a little. 'I'll take care of you.'

I pulled a face. 'Take care of me? Am I not capable of taking care of myself? I am not your property.'

'I will support you until you find another job.'

'No!'

'No?'

He placed his hand over his head as if he'd forgotten something. 'It's been bothering me for quite a while now.'

I searched his face. 'What's been bothering you?'

'Davian, he's a problem too. I think he's the biggest problem of them all. I come to surprise my girlfriend and find her alone with him in the copy room in an empty office!'

I crossed my hands beneath my chest. 'We are co-workers.'

Abdel took a step closer to me, his face tight, his jaw clenched. I'd never seen him like this, so jealous and insecure.

'Is that what you tell yourself, you two are co-workers?'

I drop my hands to my side. 'There is nothing going on between me and Anthony or Davian. I'm with you, aren't I?'

'Yeah, as a substitute.'

'What is that supposed to mean?'

He looked across the empty street. 'I saw the way you look at Davian. I can give you the moon and you never look at me that way.'

'That's not true.'

'You can lie to me, but you can't lie to yourself.' He lowered his head. 'I can't do this. I'm sorry, but I can't.'

'Abdel, I...'

I attempted to take a step towards him, but he stopped me. 'Don't, it's over.'

Tears prickled. 'No, no.'

He walked backwards. 'You can have both of them now.'

'But I want you.'

'Goodbye, Lottie.'

I watched him walk out of my life, watched the closeness replacing itself with distance. I kept on watching. Hoping he'd change his mind and turn around and tell me he was sorry, he didn't mean it, but the darkness swallowed him, leaving me shaking with tears. Lilia came out.

'Lottie, honey, what's wrong?' she asked, placing her hand on my back.

I wrapped my arms around her. 'It's over.'

'What's over?'

'Abdel, he dumped me,' I said between sobs.

A volcanic heat rushed into me and it twirled into my beating, aching heart. I attempted to push past Lilia, but she held me by the shoulder. I had to find Davian, confront him, cause a scene, and fling a drink in his perfect, stupid face. I hated him.

'Let me go!' I shouted.

'And if I do? What are you going to do?'

'Have a word with him.' My blood boiled, it steamed into my face, making my head explode, 'Davian did this. He said something to Abdel.'

'He's not worth it, let him be.'

'Let him be!' I said. 'He just ruined my relationship! I'll ruin his too and see how he feels about that!'

She shook me as mascara smudged all over my eyes. My chest quivered as big fat tears came pouring out of me. 'I'll take you home, but you're not going in there or anywhere near Davian.'

'Where is Anthony?'

'He left, apparently. His girlfriend wasn't too happy with you.'

***

As for Oli, she dumped me on the spot. She wasn't going to take this bullshit, trying to compete with a girl who obviously has my heart, as Oli had put it. The next day, I woke up as if I had a massive hangover, although I'd hardly had a drink at the party. I found twenty missed calls from Lottie. She was the last person I wanted to talk to. Another five missed calls from Davian. I didn't want to talk to him, either. Ella called. I took her call and she told me Lottie had been dumped and she was a mess. She must have thought about the outcome before pulling that stunt in front of everyone. Did I blame Abdel? No, she had it coming. The guy was patient with her. I didn't understand why she had to ruin my relationship in the process.

Chapter Seventeen

I jolt upright. It was morning, and I had fallen asleep on the kitchen table. There is a plate from last night, with the overflowing ashtray and dirty mugs. The memories of the party came strong and hard. I rub my sore neck, make myself a cup of coffee and continue where I left off.

***

Lottie's Recordings. Clip Twelve

I went to work and returned to an empty home. I haven't heard from Abdel and I made no attempts to call. I don't think he wanted to hear from me. Davian didn't show his face, which was for the best. I wasn't sure what I'd do if I saw him. Giselle locked herself in the office, and sometimes she sent me to buy supplies for the next exhibition, which is Davian's. She must have heard what happened, but she didn't question me, not that I expect her to. Giselle is my boss. What matters to her is that I do my job and do it right. I called Anthony hundreds of times, but my calls went unanswered. My apartment feels like a tomb; the mail holds no letters of any significance or importance, and I'm single again. I have caused this. I brought this on myself. Davian has nothing to do with this; no, he does, and he shouldn't have said what he said. It's easier to blame him, to put a fault on someone else. A few days before Davian's big exhibition, I met Ella for a drink.

'Why don't you quit?' she suggested.

The question seemed so foreign to me. Quit for what? Because of a guy? If he had an issue with me working there, it was his problem. Giselle liked me enough, why should I leave?

'You're saying how unbearable it has become to work there, and Davian is responsible for breaking you and Abdel up. I wouldn't want to work there if I were in your shoes. This Davian sounds like a scumbag,' Ella went on.

I took a sip of wine. 'I have bills to pay. I can't just quit.'

'I'm not telling you to quit without a job. Be sensible, you apply for jobs. When a position is offered and everything is agreed, then you slap in the notice. Anyone will hire you in no time knowing you worked for Giselle. I know Anthony found you the job, but he won't hold it against you if you find something better. He'd do the same.'

***

I would have understood. I didn't expect her to work there forever. It was only temporary until she got her feet on the ground. I don't think she wanted to leave, not because she liked to work there, but because of Davian. She was a masochistic romantic who thought something would blossom between her and him. It's worrying and disturbing seeing how deep her infatuation was.

As if Davian was going to leave the safety and security he has with Melissa and discard that familiarity to be with Lottie. She might have been my best friend, but to Davian, she was the unknown. I don't think that Davian was attracted to Lottie. In his eyes she was just another pretty girl who had a crush on him.

Chapter Eighteen

Lottie's funeral is going to be held tomorrow at 3:00 pm at Christ Church in Richmond. Her mum just called to deliver the news.

I sit on the chair and bury my face on my hands and let it crash over me. I tried to deny it, believe that this had been a bad dream, wake up from it, and she'd be alive. That she would show up and say *I got you this time* as if all of this was a practical joke.

***

Lottie's Recordings. Clip Thirteen

I had a few drinks across the street from the gallery before I built up enough courage to go in the exhibition. I got in with no hassle. The portraits hang on the wall, but I didn't bother to stop and admire them. I had one thing in mind. To find the son of a bitch and give him a piece of my mind.

Oriental chill-out music played in the background, making the atmosphere as if I were in some exotic location. I spotted him looking pristine in a checked blazer, with not a hair out of place. He was talking to a couple and I almost changed my mind. What was I going to gain from this anyway? All I had to do was turn before he saw me and walk out. No, I'm not going to let him get away with it; he wrecked my relationship. I scanned the room to see if Melissa was there. She wasn't. Weird, I thought, why she wouldn't be there for her boyfriend's exhibition to offer her moral support. I took a glass of wine from the passing waiter. Davian did a double-take. He said something to the couple and marched towards me.

'What the hell are you doing here?' he hissed.

'You know why?' I said, draining my glass and taking another from the waiter.

'This is not the time,' he said, his eyes darting across the room.

'No? It's never the right time, is it? You crashed my party. Now I'm going to crash yours.'

'God damn it!' he snarled.

'How dare you? How could you?' I said, now raising my voice.

'This is so immature and stupid. Grow up, will you?'

A few heads turned in our direction. Giselle hurried towards us.

'What do you two think you're doing arguing in front of our clients? I'm trying to run a business here, not a circus!' she said through greeted teeth.

'She's not supposed to be here,' Davian said.

Giselle turned on her heel. 'I've had enough of this. You two need to sort out whatever issues you have. Follow me now before I fire you both!'

We followed her to the lift. 'It's not the time or place to do this,' Giselle said.

'Just sack her,' Davian said.

I looked at him. 'I'd bet you can't wait for that to happen.'

'Stop this and behave like adults!' Giselle said.

The lift opened and we were back in the offices. Giselle jiggled a set of keys in her hand as we followed her. She stopped in front of a white door and opened it, pointing her finger at the room.

'In,' she hissed.

It was an unoccupied office. There was a glass desk with an empty vase on top of it, and a large window overlooking the city skyline. Davian and I stepped in but Giselle stood by the door.

'Now, if you kids will excuse me, I have business to attend to,' she said, closing the door behind her.

'You had some nerve showing up here,' Davian said with a tone as cold as ice.

'Why?' I asked.

'Why what?' he said.

'Why did you do that?'

'I didn't do anything. It was done by your hand. He saw with his own eyes.'

'How can you stand there and say this? You made it worse!' I was shouting now.

'Look, I don't have time for this,' he said. *'I have people waiting for me, and I would like to show my face in there.'*

He turned to the door.

'Shut the fucking door!' I yelled, rushing over to block his way. *'You are so arrogant; do you realise what you have done? You ruined everything.'*

'Then go and fix it!' he shouted back.

'How would you feel if I went to your darling Melissa and told her you are shagging someone else?'

He chortled. 'She wouldn't believe you.'

'That's not the point. How would you feel?' I screamed at his face.

***

I don't know what she tried to prove by doing this. Giselle could have fired her, going after her most respected photographer on the day of his exhibition. It didn't fix things, and Abdel wasn't going to change his mind. It was childish, immature and unprofessional on her part. Letting her personal emotions get in the way of her work. She should have done what Ella told her in the first place: quit and move on. Lottie didn't tell me about this, but I'm not surprised. She had kept things from me, lied to me, so many times. Davian didn't tell me about this either. Giselle must have done everything in her power to make this go unnoticed with the staff so they wouldn't gossip about it: the photographer and the assistant in the screaming match.

At the time, I locked myself in the flat and mended my broken heart with work while Lottie tried to win the battle but not the war. I did confront Davian; like hell, I was going to let this one slide. I had a couple of drinks at a pub not far from his apartment before I went pounding on his door.

'What's wrong with you?' I said after he opened the door. 'Seriously, mate, what's the matter with you?'

'Are you drunk?' he asked coolly.

'No, I'm not drunk, but you don't go around and tell people lies.'

His face remained expressionless. 'Lies? I wasn't lying. Everyone saw, mate.'

'Yes, but what you said to him made it much worse! Not only did Oli break up with me, you made it awkward between Lottie and I. Abdel broke up with her. He thinks we are lovers, thanks to your big mouth.'

He ran his fingers through his hair. 'Look, I've done nothing wrong. All I did was have a chat with the guy.'

'It was an arsehole move, Davian,' I said, and slammed the door behind me.

***

His blue eyes bore into mine, his jaw tight. He moved away from the door, cursing under his breath. He turned to face me, keeping his distance.

'You are not going to get away with this. I'm going to make sure you never set foot in this building ever again. Anthony is a saint for helping you get this job. Thanks for ruining my evening, by the way.'

'And you ruined my life.'

'I ruined your life? God, you're dramatic, stupid and weak.'

His words stabbed me. 'I'm not stupid nor weak.'

'Oh yes, you are, look at you. You blame me for something you did because it's much easier that way, isn't it?'

'You're a cruel man with an ugly heart,' I said.

'Say what you want. It won't affect me. We can be here all night and it won't change anything.'

All I wanted was for him to apologise, but it wasn't going to happen. This man is not going to admit his wrongdoings.

'Go home, Lottie,' he said, waving his hand away as if I was some bug that was bothering him. 'You're hurt. Go get a terrible haircut, eat ice cream or whatever silly girls like you do.'

'What have I done to you to cause this contempt? This resentment?' I said, my voice breaking.

'Shut up.'

'Don't tell me to shut up.'

He looked up at the ceiling. 'Great, she's crying now.'

He took a step closer to me and placed his hand on the small of my back.

'Why do you hate me so much?' I asked.

'I don't hate you, Lottie.' His voice was slow and soothing.

'Then why?' I said, hot tears streaming down my face. 'I lost a friend because of you.'

'Anthony will come around. He just needs time. He's not the type who would abandon his friends.'

His face was soft now. 'Look, let's forget this ever happened. I'll tell Giselle we worked out our issues and you just need some time off.'

'You're not going to make her fire me?'

'No, I'm not. I promise.'

I reached for the collar of his jacket. His perfume wrestled its way to my nose, intoxicating me.

'Why don't you say that you're sorry for everything?'

'Lottie, let me go,' he said in a firm tone, as if I were a child.

I held on tighter to his jacket. I wanted to let go, leave and go home and never show my face in there ever again. Everything I touch turns into shit. He seized my hand.

***

There is a pause on the clip. For a moment, I think it's finished, but there are a few minutes left. What is it, Lottie? What happened in that office? She comes into view again. Her eyes are lowered. She bites her bottom lip, tears streaming down her cheeks. My heart sinks. What did he do to her?

***

He pushed me by the wall. He tried to kiss me.
'What are you doing?' I demanded.
'What you always wanted,' he said.
His lips were hot against mine.

***

That son of a bitch!

***

'Davian... it's not right.'
'I don't care.'

His hand worked on the waistband of my panties and lowered them to my ankles.

'Davian...'

'I don't care, I don't care,' he said over and over.

The room spun; all the anger and venom was gone. We moved to the desk. I removed his tie and jacket. He undid his belt and my brain wobbled. I couldn't believe this was happening. I heard something crash on the floor, but that didn't stop us as he took me.

***

I shut the laptop with my mouth hanging open. My skin tingling. I'm speechless. Does that mean...? But... Davian is the other man? I rise to my feet and pour myself a glass of vodka. I can't stand it, the two of them lying to my face. I'm so angry and betrayed, I want to bite the table. I can't listen to this gibberish. He had a girlfriend. Lottie was cheating with him. This made her the other woman. I thought she was better than this. It turns out, I didn't know her at all. She's a stranger. Tomorrow is her funeral, and here I am listening to this! If Giselle hears about this, she'll hit the roof. Lottie's voice rambled in my head.

God, it was so hot. It was the best few minutes of my life.

The best few minutes of her life? Jesus. Mary. Joseph. Shame on you, Lottie. Shame on you,

Davian. Just colleagues, yeah right. How am I supposed to face Davian knowing this?

Chapter Nineteen

My hands are shaking so much, I can't do my tie. Giving up, I sit on the edge of the bed and light a cigarette. The buzzer goes off. Ella called me yesterday to arrange to meet me here so we can go together to the funeral. The flat is in disarray, with empty plates on the table and mugs in the sink. The furniture needs dusting, clothes are tossed on the bedroom floor. Ella places the umbrella by the door, walks over and gives me a hug. She is not wearing any make-up and I'm still holding the tie in my hand.

'I can't... do my tie. Will you do it for me?' I ask her.

'Of course.'

I watch her hands doing the knot. For a moment, I want to tell her everything, about the laptop, the videos, that Lottie was sexually involved with Davian. I can't carry this burden alone. This secret. Ella's eyes go up to my face. I open my mouth hoping the words will come out. My body spasms. It feels as if something heavy has landed on me.

'You're shaking,' she says.

'I'm cold.'

That's all I manage to say.

The casket stands in front of the altar surrounded with flowers. I don't think I would be able to handle it, knowing that inside it lay her body, soon to be buried. She died alone and helpless. I heave as I stand by the coffin and place my hand on the wood; no matter what type of wood it is, it's still a box, and she is in it. My friend that I have known, cared for and loved. The friend that lied and kept secrets from me. As if I meant nothing, as if our friendship meant nothing. It's not her in that coffin, not Lottie. Her corpse is in there but what about the rest of her?

'Why you didn't tell me? Why did you feel the need to speak to a laptop instead of talking to me?' I sigh. 'I'm going to find out who did this to you.'

I sit in the second row, Ella beside me. In the front row are Lottie's parents and family members. There is a picture of Lottie, one I have never seen before; she's sitting in the park smiling prettily at the camera. She looks so innocent and pure. I wipe the tears away. The church is slowly filling up. The priest appears and opens the Bible, the organ starts and the people rise.

During the ceremony, I scanned the church; Giselle and Lilia were sitting in another row. Behind them is Abdel. I nod at him and he does the same. Lilia nods I nod back. There are my mum and my dad. Dad sees me and I nod. At the far back, standing, is Davian. Melissa is nowhere in sight. Davian is leaning against the pillar, his hands shoved in his trouser pocket, gazing ahead, too wrapped up in his own thoughts to see me looking at him.

The wake is held at Lottie's parents'. Her mum comes over and gives me a hug, and I shake her father's hand.

'Thank you for coming,' her father says.

He turns and leaves the room. Emily places her hand to mine. 'I'm sorry, he's still in shock.'

'I understand. Is there anything I can help you with Mrs... er, Emily?'

'No, it's quite all right, dear.'

My parents enter the house. They come over and offer their condolences to Emily.

'Are you all right, love?' my mum asks.

I nod.

Dad towers over me. 'I'm sorry, son. She was a special girl.'

Apart from being sneaky and secretive, yeah, she was special, I think bitterly.

'Yes, she was,' I say.

I wonder what will happen if I show Lottie's parents the laptop, to see their daughter come to life. They have every right to know. My mum goes to the kitchen to help with the food.

'Your mum told me the police came over to the house to ask about you,' my dad says.

'Yes, she told me.'

'I wish she'd called before talking to them.'

I look at him, at this man who saw me as a burden. Too wrapped up in his anger to spend time with me. Always working, always tired. The slaps I got from him. He might think I don't remember, but I do. Every child remembers; it leaves a mark, an imprint.

'What difference would it have made? I have nothing to hide, Dad.' I say.

I scan the room. Abdel is nowhere to be seen, nor Giselle and Lilia. Davian walks in. He scans the house, spots me and heads in our direction.

'I'll go and check on your mother,' my dad says, and motions to the kitchen.

'Anthony,' Davian says.

Why every time he appears, the room becomes icy?

'Davian.'

He is my friend who I have known for years; we grew up together, we stood side by side, we laughed and fought, and I have nothing to say. I can't just pretend I don't know what I discovered. I will never look at him the same way.

'Where is Melissa?'

'She's stayed behind. She didn't know Lottie very well.'

Or she knew what he was doing behind her back and threw him on his arse. Emily is holding a tray of sandwiches, staring at Davian. Is she wondering who he is, or does she know who he is? She can't seem to keep her eyes off him while passing the sandwiches around. From the look on her face, I can see she's not happy. What the hell is going on? Why does he look so nervous? Has he been in this house before? Did Lottie bring him here? Has he met her parents? Been introduced as her boyfriend when he wasn't?

'It was a nice ceremony,' I say, trying to ease the pressure.

'Yes, it was.'

'Are you…?'

The loud clatter in the room makes me jump. I glance over my shoulder. Emily is staring at a tray of sandwiches scattered all over the floor. My mum runs to her.

'I'll be right back,' I say to Davian.

'I'm going for a smoke,' he said.

Emily is sitting at the kitchen table with a glass of water.

'I'll take it from here. You stay put, okay, love?' my mum says to Emily.

God bless my mum for helping out. I take a canapé from the tray before my mom walks out of the room.

'That young man you were talking to, who is he?' Emily said in a quiet tone.

'That's Davian, he's a friend. He used to work with Lottie.'

Emily stands and goes to the sink, looking out of the window. Davian's back is facing the window, smoking and texting.

'I've seen him before,' Emily says.

Chapter Twenty

We continue to look at Davian from the kitchen window. It's unlikely she saw Davian in a magazine or in an art exhibition. I didn't take her for the type who reads those sorts of things.

'Where?' I ask, unable to mask my shock.

She eyes me wryly and sits down on the chair. 'What does he do?'

I lean against the counter. 'He's a photographer.'

She nods. 'The two detectives came over again and asked me if Lottie ever mentioned a colleague named Davian.'

'Did she?'

'No, she didn't.'

I sit down across from her. 'Where did you see him?'

'Here.'

'Here?'

'Outside the house, a few months ago. Lottie came to spend the weekend. I had a headache and I went to lie down. At some point, I went to the window and I saw her talking to that attractive young man. She was pointing her finger at him. I suppose they were arguing. A few minutes later, she walked away from him then I heard the front door slam and the shower running. Later, I asked her who the man was and she got all cross and accused me of spying on her.'

Why had Davian come here? What were they arguing about?

'And you told this to the police?'

Emily gives me a strange look. 'I didn't know it was him, the young man I saw here, so no, I didn't tell them.'

Davian is in a lot more trouble than he thinks he is.

'Is he a bad man?' Emily asks.

'No,' I said.

Although, now I feel I don't know Davian at all or what he's capable of.

Davian hands me his lighter to fire up my cigarette and we smoke in silence, staring at the houses.

'The police want to talk to me again.'

'They do?' I asked.

'Yes, they want me to go to the police station tomorrow morning. I'm going with my solicitor.'

I could picture him striding into the police station, groomed within an inch of his life. Alongside him would be a hotshot solicitor, provided by Giselle of course. Davian can't afford a hotshot lawyer. I wonder where Davian was when Lottie was murdered. It seems everything is linked to him.

'A solicitor, huh?' I say, puffing on my cigarette.

'Yeah, whatever I say can be used as evidence.'

I give him a sideways glance and he shakes his head. 'I don't know why they want to interview me again. I told them what I know.'

Did he tell them he had sex with her? Did the police find out the truth behind their relationship?

Is this why they want him to go down to the police station? Knowing him, how reserved he is, he would leave the sex part out. To save himself any form of embarrassment or from Melissa finding out.

'It's standard procedure. The police will interview anyone who was in contact with Lottie, even co-workers.' I mash the cigarette under my shoe and light another one.

'Did they tell you to go down the station?' he asked.

'No, they didn't.'

'So, you don't understand my concern,' he says seriously.

'Davian, if the police want to arrest you, they wouldn't be so formal about it.'

'Yes, but I have no alibi, that's why.'

I turn to him, but I don't say anything.

'I was at my apartment all evening. I wanted to come to your exhibition, but I got held up with work.'

I'm not offended about Davian not coming to my exhibition. I hardly went to his anyway, but I'd invited him to come if he wanted to. Davian didn't like to go out that much. My friend is rather odd.

'Where was Melissa?' I asked.

'She was in Japan. I went to pick her up the day after.'

'Oh yes, you told me.'

Dread fills my stomach and leaves me hollow. I need to go back to the clips to see if this escalated into an affair. What if Lottie wanted him to leave Melissa? What if she threatened him? Despite my trepidation, I'm not going to accuse him of anything, not until he's proven guilty.

'Is Abdel a suspect?' Davian asks.

'Why would he be? They broke up months before she... died.'

'Jealousy, I suppose,' Davian says, looking down at his lighter.

'Of whom?' I say. 'She was single. She wasn't seeing anyone... at least not that we know of.'

Davian doesn't blink. A couple walks out of the house and we keep quiet until they have passed.

'It's a crime of passion,' he says.

A crime of passion; how about that? He fires another cigarette. 'The thing is you never know with people,' he continues.

'Indeed, you don't,' I agree.

People work in mysterious ways. Here is a guy who I knew, at least that's what I thought. I don't expect that he would tell me everything, same with Lottie, but lie about it? They made a deal that made them both liars.

'This is a nice neighbourhood, don't you think?' I ask.

Now he gives me a sideways glance, 'Yeah, I suppose.'

'Have you been here before?'

'No.'

Another lie. One of many. What is he hiding?

I take a deep drag from my cigarette, unable to hold it any longer.

'I know.'

'You know what?'

I see his iciness melting away. I give it to him in simple English.

'I know about you and Lottie.'

Chapter Twenty-One

I'm dying to hear what he has to say, now that he been caught lying to me all along. He gives me a sharp glance.

'And what do you think you know?' he asked, his voice sharp as steel.

'You had sex with her.'

Is he going to deny it? I throw the cigarette on the pavement. 'She was my best friend.'

'Yeah, and so am I.'

'So, are you going to deny it?' I ask, searching his face.

'Yes, I am, because what you think happened, or whatever she told you, it's not true.'

'Jesus, Davian, your mistress was murdered?'

He takes a step closer. 'Lottie wasn't my...' he pauses, takes a deep breath, this must be a lot to take in for both of us.

'I didn't know she would be killed now, did I?' He runs his hand through his hair. 'When did she tell you this? Why have you waited so long to tell me? I thought you were my friend.'

'I am your friend, Davian.'

'Let me guess,' he says, throwing the cigarette on the ground. 'She told you we were having an affair. I know you were fond of her, but Lottie wasn't what you think she was. She was a pathological liar.'

'No, Davian. You don't get to blame her because she's dead and she's no longer around to defend herself, and don't go around calling her a liar.'

'Fine. You want to take her side? Go ahead,' Davian hissed.

'I'm not taking sides. My friend was murdered and I'm trying to figure out why.'

'Lottie might have acted like she was this good girl, but it was all a facade, Anthony. She was making stuff up about me, as I suspected, and she told you too. How long have you known?'

'What stuff? Know what?'

'That we were having an affair, which we weren't.'

If she was making stuff up about him, how come I never heard about it? Why was he keeping it a secret? Why didn't he tell me?

'But you had sex with her?'

'No, I didn't.'

I search his face. He doesn't blink once nor break eye contact. I think he's telling the truth. What about those videos? Were they lies? Why would Lottie spend so much time recording herself telling lies? That would be ludicrous and insane.

'How come you never told me?'

'I had it under control.'

'Did you have it under control? Did you tell the police any of this?'

'Of course, I didn't; it would make me a suspect. Which I'm getting the impression I already am.' He looks across the street. 'I swear, it's not what it looks like.'

'I know you. I know you're not a killer,' I assure him, or is it myself I am assuring?

What about Lottie? Was she really making stuff up about him? Now that I'm beginning to learn her secrets, nothing would shock me. A few more guests come out of the house. Ella is standing by the door and frowns at me. Davian glances back to see at who I am looking at and it hits me. It's like a piano falls over my head.

'Of course,' I say aloud.

Davian draws his eyebrows together. 'What?'

'I have to go,' I say.

I walk past him towards the house to offer my goodbyes. I run into Ella on my way out.

'Where are you going?'

'There is someplace I have to be.'

'Right now?' she asks.

'Yes, I'll be in touch,' I say, giving her hug and running out of the house.

I rush home and switch on the laptop.

'Come on, come on,' I say to it as it loads up.

I go to the protected folder and I suck in a breath and type.

The most beautiful man on earth.

Chapter Twenty-Two

It was how Lottie described Davian after all, the prettiest man she had ever seen. Now I am beginning to understand how deep her obsession with Davian truly was. I shudder as if a spider is crawling on my back. It's rather creepy to see all of this in front of me, and she hid it from everyone.

There are photos of him taken from magazines, articles about him or related to him that she gathered from the internet. Photos taken in groups at exhibitions or parties. There is a group photo taken at a staff party; Davian is standing next to Giselle while Lottie is at the back. I zoom in and she's looking at him, not at the camera. Photos she must have taken on her phone of his work. What draws my attention are the Post-its. No messages. Just a time. This was his way to communicate with her to have their trysts, and this was the evidence of that. Where did they meet? At her place? Was there a hotel? I banged my hand against the table. The liar! He denied having an affair with her, when there was all of this in front of me?

What you think happened, or whatever she told you, it's not true, he had said.

I wish I could go back and shove this laptop in his face. What would he say? That she wrote them herself? It's his handwriting, italic and messy. I would know it anywhere. I can't stand the lies, the deceit, and the betrayal. I want to bang my head against the table and hope this will be over. This laptop has enough evidence to incriminate him.

Besides the photos, Post-its and the letters, there is an audio clip. I click on it and the player pops up. There are muffling sounds, followed by sighs and moans. I rub my face, did she actually? I'm speechless.

I punch the stop button. I've heard and seen enough. This is madness! It makes me question her sanity. Was her obsession stretched so far that she couldn't think straight? What would Davian say if he had to listen to this? He'd be furious. Climb up the bloody wall, that's what he'll do. He would never ever allow her to record this. She recorded their lovemaking behind his back, edited out the unnecessary bits, and kept what she thought was useful. She might even have planned it. What for? What had she planned to do with this recording? Go to Melissa with it and expose him? Was she threatening him? She might even go as far as blackmailing him if he didn't do what she required of him. I can take a guess what that might have been, to have him all to herself.

All of us pass through a shop occasionally and stop dead in our tracks to take a second look at an item we like. We admire it then we look at the price and we scowl. It's something we can't afford. Some of us save up for it, and some of us move on. That's what Lottie's relationship with Davian was, the expensive item in a shop display that she couldn't afford but wanted to have, no matter what the cost, even steal to obtain it. He wasn't the object of her affection anymore, not even a man made of flesh and blood, but an accessory. We, her friends, were so oblivious of what she was doing. If I'd known, I would have done everything in my power to stop her. But she kept it to herself, only sharing it with a laptop. To him, she must have become a burden he regretted. Why didn't he tell me about this either? This is serious. Did he do the unthinkable and get rid of her because he failed to see another alternative? I refused to believe it.

I step away from the laptop and lie on the bed, staring at the ceiling, trying to find a meaning in of all of this. One man, an obsession, one dead girl.

I drift off and wake up in the dark. Someone is shouting under my window. I get up on my feet and look out to see a couple arguing, a woman in a red coat and a bloke in a leather jacket. The woman slaps him across the cheek and stomps off. I go to the kitchen and inspect the mess.

'Right,' I say to myself.

I start to scrub the counters until my hands begin to ache, my mind racing. The police suspect she knew the killer. Did Lottie give Davian a key to her apartment? No, I know him. He wouldn't do such a thing. I'm disgusted at myself for thinking this.

***

Lottie's Recordings. Clip Fourteen

I was mortified. I was so confused. This man never showed any interest in me. I didn't know what to think. How am I going to face him after this? I left through the fire exit and ran down the stairs. What have I done? What if Melissa finds out? I pushed the door open and I could breathe again.

It was a shitty thing to do. How dare I do such a thing? Is this what I have become? He had a girlfriend, whom he adored, and I'm responsible for his infidelity. I hid under the covers listening to the sounds, the ticking of the clock on the bedside table. Someone put the music on. Michael Bolton's voice boomed through the walls. It seemed my neighbours were about to get their groove on. I buried my head under the pillow as the events replayed in my mind. His hair soft on my hands, his lips like silk. I wanted to stay tucked under the covers and never come out.

I could have stayed in bed, but not when there are responsibilities. I had to continue as if nothing happened. I couldn't look at my face in the mirror, how could I ever? I washed my face, avoiding catching glimpses of myself so I didn't have to face my indignity. I met Ella for lunch and I let her do most of the talking. I should have cancelled. I was terrible company. I kept thinking what would happen if he invented a fictional story to have me fired. After what happened, I'm sure he doesn't want to see me again. Facing me at work would be unbearable. Maybe I should start looking for a new job.

Ella asked me if I was feeling all right. I stared at her and I thought of telling her what had happened with Davian. I would watch her eyes go wide. I would watch her shock as she demanded I tell her everything.

I shrugged. 'I'm still getting over the breakup.'

She gave me a sympathetic look, which made me want to run away. 'Everything will be fine. I know it doesn't look that way right now, but it will.'

I loved her for her optimism.

I called Anthony, but the phone rang and rang and he never picked up.

On Monday, I walked into the office with my heart in my mouth. My eyes darted at the staff to see if they were staring at me, but everyone was focused on their work. Lilia was in the kitchen making peppermint tea.

'You look grey,' she said, placing a gentle hand on my forearm. 'Are you feeling all right?'

I wanted to be sick. I told her I'm still getting over the breakup. In return, I got a hug.

I kept myself occupied trying to put the episode behind me. I didn't see him. I suspected he was working from home. I didn't want to see him, not yet, not ever.

I didn't join Lilia for lunch. I was on my way to make myself a cup of coffee when Giselle walked out of her office. She looked at me and a man walked over to have a word with her. I hurried to the kitchen; she knows, I thought. My heart thumped against my chest. Davian must have told her something that will get me sacked. After what happened, Davian had to go back to his exhibition, put on a brave face and get on with the evening. Giselle would have demanded a progress report.

I opened the packet of digestive biscuits. As I munched on my biscuits, the phone rang. I stared at the phone as if it was a bomb about to go off.

'Giselle wants to talk to you ASAP,' Taylor said.

The biscuits grew like cotton wool in my mouth and swallowing was a struggle. Davian had said he wouldn't tell Giselle to sack me, but he hadn't kept his promise. Why would he? Just because he was inside me didn't give me any sense of entitlement. The man wants me out and he's going to get it. My knees shook as I wobbled to her office. Giselle sat behind her desk.

'You wanted to see me?' I asked, trying to keep my voice steady.

'Lottie, yes. Please, close the door,' she said firmly without looking at me. 'Have a seat.'

I felt a rush going through my face as I sat down waiting for it to come out. Pack your shit and get out!

'I've heard you and Davian are friends now,' she told me in a bright tone.

Is this why she summoned me, to get a progress report from me too? My heart slowed. So, I'm not going to get the sack? He kept to his word; maybe fucking him gave me some sort of privilege. No, we are not friends. What does this makes us? Lovers? I can hardly call it that. It happened once.

'Um... er...'

Forming words seemed like an effort.

'He told me on his way out, you made up. I'm pleased.'

I gripped the chair. On his way out? So, he was here? But I didn't see him and I'm the last person he wants to see right now. I'm sure he must be hiding in his office and won't come out until he's done.

'Well... sort of,' I said, as heat swam to my face.

'My... you are flushed. Are you all right?'

'Yes, I'm fine.'

'How are things with you in general? I've heard about you and Abdel. I'm sorry. If you need anything, someone to talk to, my office is open.'

When I returned to my cubical, I spotted a pink Post-it, which wasn't there when I left. I blinked at it in disbelief.

Meet me over the arch in Bermondsey Street at 8:00 pm, tonight.

PS Bring this note with you.

D

I stared at it until the words blurred.

***

Is this how the affair started? Why the railway station?

Chapter Twenty-Three

I'm too jittery to sleep. I want to find out as much as possible, the sooner I do this, the sooner I'll get to move on with my life. I pour myself a shot of vodka and pass several glances at the computer as if it's poison. I need to find a way to hand this over to the police, but I don't want to worry about that right now.

***

Lottie's Recordings. Clip Fifteen

I headed over to the arch on Bermondsey Street; it was spooky meeting him there. He was leaning against the brick wall. He's so beautiful and I had him for a while.

'Hi,' I said.

'Hi.'

He didn't lean over to kiss me; I was hoping he would.

'Did you bring the note?' he asked.

I took it out from my jacket pocket and handed it to him. He took it and shoved it in his pocket.

'What is this about?'

'We need to talk.'

'I suppose we do,' I said.

We walked side by side, not talking. How can a man and a woman share such passion, such intensity and fire, and dissolve into nothing? Like the dying of a flame. There was a gang of young people talking too loudly, too absorbed in themselves, to pay any attention to us. He hailed a taxi. We didn't talk in there either. I wanted him to take me to his place and repeat what happened before. The drive, however, was to a restaurant.

Did he and Melissa break up?

Candles and flowers sat on the ivory tablecloths. A man in a tuxedo walked over, offering to take our coats. A warning would have been nice to dress more appropriately instead of office clothes. We were ushered to a table in the far back where the lights were dimmer. The man gave us the menu and asked if we'd like to order drinks. A glass of champagne, perhaps? I didn't know why, but it sounded so offensive. A glass of champagne would have been nice in a different situation, on a different occasion, but this wasn't a cause for celebration.

'Water is fine...' Davian paused and glanced at me. 'Still or sparkling?'

'Anything, it's fine,' I replied.

'Still, please,' Davian said.

'Room temperature or cold?' the man asked.

For a moment, I thought the man was going to hover there and ask us, do we want it from the tap? From the bottle? What sort plastic or glass? Evian or San Pellegrino? I wanted the man to go away so I would discover the reason for this dinner. Why such a fancy place? Why not in a casual restaurant? Is this what Davian liked? Dining in swanky restaurants that cost a fortune? We were so different, him and I. Davian sure liked his luxury. He dined like a fine gentleman, spent another fortune on his hair and clothes. Is this what he and Melissa did together? It seemed so dull, so pedestrian. We were worlds apart. I wrinkled my nose as if something had begun to stink. I couldn't see why he was going to this trouble. We didn't have to sit there for three hours sipping on expensive wine and eat fluffy food to establish our relationship.

'That was some apology,' he said.

My cheeks coloured.

'I'm sorry,' he said, blushing. 'How are you?'

What was he apologising for? The sex or for what he'd said. How am I? I couldn't stop thinking about him.

'I'm... okay.'

His eyes went back to the menu. 'You didn't hear from him?'

'Who?'

'Abdel.'

I lowered my head. 'No, I haven't. You know it's over. Don't ask me that.'

The man returned with our water. We stayed silent until he poured it in our glasses.

'How is Melissa?' I asked after the waiter left.

He played with the napkin. 'She's fine...'

'So, you two are still together?'

He glanced at me sharply. 'What makes you think we aren't?'

'I don't know, I suppose that we had sex and I assumed that...' I sighed, dropping the menu on the table. *'I don't know what I thought.'*

I took a quick glance at him. I couldn't read his expression. Of course, he and Melissa were still together - what made me think they weren't? He wasn't going to leave her for me. Why would he? I was the convenient shag that he felt a need to treat to a romantic meal because he felt sorry for me, or about the situation, or both. I knew why he'd brought me to this beautiful, intimate restaurant: to tell me that it was a mistake, we shouldn't do something like that ever again. It was stupid. Blah, blah, blah. Somehow, sitting there, it felt offensive; the chandelier was offensive, the tablecloths and the soft music were offensive. The water and the overpriced menu were offensive. Everything about this place was.

We should have skipped the calories and fucked. But there we were. His aloofness didn't help either. He was so snotty. I hated him. I hated this menu, I hated this fancy restaurant and I hated myself. I stood pushing back the chair.

'Where are you going?'

'Um... where is the bathroom?'

A waiter rushed to our table. 'Is the lady all right?' he asked.

Why was he referring to me in the third person? 'The bathroom?' I asked the waiter.

'Straight to the right,' the waiter said.

I reached for my bag and as I pulled it, the chair moved, making a loud scraping noise, and a few heads turned. Talk about being discreet. He shouldn't have brought me here if he wanted secrecy - what if someone saw him? Not my problem, and I didn't worry about what Melissa had to say, apart from the fact that she would kick my arse, which I'll deserve. Occupied men don't bring their... office shags to public places. The bathroom made my modest white-tiled bathroom look like a tatty public toilet by comparison. The feature wall was white with a black flowery pattern, and the rest of the walls were black with golden stripes. I rested my hand on the sink to steady myself and caught my reflection in the mirror. The thought of slipping out crossed my mind, but to do that, I had to walk past our table. Davian wasn't the kind of man you walk out on when he takes you out for dinner.

The wine sat in a bucket, two glasses already poured. I took a large gulp of wine while Davian watched me closely.

'I know you find this odd, but I'm not the kind of person who opens up easily.'

'That I noticed,' I said.

'The reason I asked you to meet me is to explain myself, since you walked out so abruptly.'

'I was confused,' I said.

'Why you didn't stop me?' he said.

'Stop you?'

'Yeah.'

'Why you didn't restrain yourself?'

He reached for the wine glass and took a large gulp. I waited for him to go on.

'You were upset and I... didn't mean to say those things to you. To hurt you. I don't think you're weak and stupid. When I saw you, I got angry and I... didn't plan for that to happen but it did and we are where we are.'

What was he trying to say?

'I don't know, is that why you behaved the way you did? Because you were angry?' I asked

'Maybe... I don't know.'

'You don't know?'

The waiter walked over to take our food order.

'We need more time,' Davian said.

The waiter nodded and went to serve another table.

'What I'm trying to say is-'

'That it was a mistake?' I say.

His eyes widened. 'It was.'

'I understand.'

'No, you don't.'

'Of course, I do; I was upset. You wanted to offer me comfort and you did. It was...'

It was what? Wrong? Lovely?

'I won't tell anyone, I promise,' I said.

That seemed to put him at ease. We ordered the food and talked about work mostly. There was no touching or kissing or anything of that sort. It was nice to sit there and talk to him. After dinner, he hailed a taxi for me. I turned to him; he took my hand and kissed me on the lips. Blinking, I got in the taxi. I rubbed my hands together and placed them inside my jacket pocket. I frowned as something crisp rubbed against my skin. A paper. It was a

Post-it to meet him on Saturday with an address scribbled down.

***

Wait, she had been at Davian's apartment? Why doesn't this ring true to me? Davian wasn't going to invite Lottie to the flat he shared with Melissa, even if she was miles away. I knew Davian to well enough to know that he wouldn't be prepared to open that side of himself to Lottie. For her to see how he lived, look at the things he owned, the books he read, the records he listened to. The possessions Melissa owned, the life they shared together; it would be like standing nude in a public place for him. Exposing himself to her like that was an access he wasn't willing to give her. Or am I wrong? Why would he tell her that what they did was wrong and then ask her to meet him again? It doesn't make any sense. No one was forcing her to go. She could have refused, left him there waiting. Now I know what followed next. She went to Westminster with sweat coursing down her back, a heart racing with adrenaline, thinking about the high and the danger of it all, that she could be caught. It was exhilarating, exciting, also scary. It was new; she had never done anything like this before with the man she for so long desired.

Chapter Twenty-Four

There are always three versions to a story: Lottie's, Davian's, and the truth. Lottie had recorded clips documenting her affair with Davian. Whilst Davian had told me he wasn't having an affair with her. He said she was making up stuff about him. If it got so bad, why didn't he tell Giselle rather than dealing with it himself? That would give him a motive. She was telling lies about him, therefore, he wanted to get rid of her. I don't know what's what anymore nor who to believe. I only want to know the truth. The laptop is on the kitchen table, and I sit across from it as if it's a girlfriend who had been waiting for me.

***

Lottie's Recordings. Clip Sixteen

I didn't see Davian for the rest of the week. Lilia asked me if I'd like to watch a movie on Saturday. I nearly said yes until I remembered the Post-it tucked away in my drawer with his address on it. Why had he invited me to go to his place? Weren't we supposed to meet at a hotel? Isn't that how this works?

On Saturday, nerves prickled all over me. I got a text from Ella asking me if I'd like to meet for drinks in the evening. I declined; I didn't want to be around anyone, especially my friends. As the time drew closer, the anticipation grew. I planned what to wear, what to say to him. I had a long bath. I never questioned what I was doing. My mind was blank. I got dressed with a certain ease. I put on perfume and lipstick. I could have taken the tube, but I took a taxi instead. While I gave the address to the cabbie, the thought came crawling into me: why had he told me what happened that night couldn't be repeated and then left me a Post-it? As the car moved forward and took me closer to him, the panic began to surge its way through me. I was terrified. I paid the driver and looked up at the tall building.

***

What?

***

The apartment was in Chelsea. How could he afford a place in one of the most expensive areas in the city? A wealthy family who provided for him, maybe? I mean, he acted like a spoilt little boy.

***

I nearly spit my tea on the screen. Chelsea? No, Davian didn't come from a wealthy family. His father is a plasterer. His mother is a housewife. There was no way his father could afford an apartment over there.

***

The doorman opened the door, greeting me with a 'good afternoon' as I walked through the white marble lobby. There was a round oak table in the middle with a vase of white roses.

***

What is she talking about? What kind of fabricated bullshit is this? No, it's all bollocks. Davian never lived in Chelsea, and he couldn't afford it. He rented a tiny apartment in Westminster and the last time I checked, there certainly wasn't a doorman nor a marble lobby or a vase with white roses. Lottie is lying. There is no apartment in Chelsea. Unless it belonged to someone he knew and he'd asked her to meet him there. My mind goes blank. I can't think of anyone who might have an apartment over there.

***

I wobbled to the corridor, fixed my hair, decided whether to smile or not and knocked on the door. Discomfort screamed through the walls. The apartment was about 3,300 square feet surrounded with windows everywhere. It was bright, elegant, and it suited him. A chandelier hung from the ceiling. There was a picture of a woman's red lips. Black marble floors along with dark furniture. I took off my jacket and dropped it on the black leather sofa. There was a smell of rosewood combined with nicotine.

***

He was fooling her; that wasn't his apartment. He lied to her, giving her this illusion. Unless Lottie was making this up.

***

There was morbid silence; my body had a memory now. Please, I wanted to beg him, just get on with it.

'Why am I here?' I said.

He smiled. 'I perfectly understand, Lottie, if you don't want...' he trailed off.

'But I thought you said...'

'I know what I said.'

'Then why?'

'Why what?'

'You asked me to meet you here.'

This apartment had no trace of a woman living in it; it didn't have that touch. Nothing suggested Melissa lived here as it seemed none of his belongings were in the apartment either.

He fixed his gaze on me. I latched to him like a bear, aggressively pushed my lips to his and wrapped my legs around him. He lost his balance and landed against the wall. I sensed his shock, but he didn't stop me. We moved to each corner of the living room with my legs still wrapped around him. He was delicious. Perfect. I drowned in his embrace. I shut my eyes, collecting each caress, and each touch went to my head.

The world outside the living room faded; all that mattered was the two of us touching, exploring each other's bodies. He laid me on the sofa and crept on top of me. I rolled on top of him and we fell on the floor.

***

I remove the headphones and rub my eyes; is this what the rest of these videos are? Sexual escapades with my best friend? I can see her obsession with him had grown. By this time, I had gone on a holiday on my own to broaden my horizons. I've read somewhere if you travel alone, you learn how to enjoy your own company. I went to France, Greece, Rome, Spain and Portugal. I never called Lottie. I didn't want to speak to her. I wasn't ready. I wasn't hiding; no, I was. Meanwhile, she was busy shagging Davian. So much for mending a broken heart. Abdel was long forgotten. How did she get back with him? I wasn't there in this part of her life. The buzzer pierced through the silence and made me jump, nearly 11:00 pm. Who could it be at this hour? Davian?

Chapter Twenty-Five

My apartment becomes a cheap hotel with people coming and going. I open the front door as Giselle comes up the stairs, her heels clicking on the steps.

'Anthony, do you have a moment?' she asks, sliding past me.

'Sure,' I say, shutting the door.

She looks around and I stretch the back of my neck.

'Can I offer you a cup of tea?' I ask her timidly.

'You have anything stronger?' she demands.

'I'll see what I can find.'

She places her expensive bag on the sofa and settles down, crossing her long brown legs. It feels awkward having her here.

'I suppose you heard,' she says.

'Heard what?' I ask, looking over my shoulder.

She cast me a look, as if I had been hiding under a rock these past twenty-four hours. She produces her phone from her bag, taps on the screen and shows it to me. I squint at the screen. The headline comes like a punch, each blow so powerful it kicks and kicks. Acid rises through my throat. Lottie, murder, arrest. Davian taken into custody. I slump on the sofa.

'Davian had been taken to custody? Why?'

'He's a suspect in her murder,' Giselle says.

'Davian a suspect? But-'

'Did you know about him and Lottie?' she asks.

'What?'

'Don't play dumb with me. Did you or didn't you know Davian and Lottie were having an affair? They were your friends after all.'

Her annoyance echoes on the walls. So Davian was lying; there was an affair. If the police found out about it, it has to be true. The police base things on the evidence; it doesn't mean it's the truth because of that. Innocent people go to prison all the time. What did they find? I stand up, my legs wobbling under me and my heart beating so fast, I'm sure Giselle can hear it. I reach for the bottle of vodka and place it on the coffee table, along with two tumblers.

'I have no ice. Sorry,' I say, non-apologetically.

She reaches for the bottle. 'It will do.'

I can't lie to her, but I don't know what she's trying to get out of me. Am I fired?

'I had no idea. No,' I say.

She pours vodka into the tumbler. 'There is enough evidence to link the murder to Davian. Apparently they found items in her apartment.'

'What kind of items?'

'His clothes.'

The police found Davian's clothes in Lottie's apartment? He was going to hers as well? Why would he leave clothes at her place? Davian is too orderly to do something this reckless. He might have been having an affair with her and lying to me about it, but something doesn't feel right.

'They did?'

How does Giselle know about all of this?

'How do you know?' The question comes out before I can stop myself.

She stands and smooths the invisible creases from her white pencil skirt.

'Money buys you friends, and friends of friends. It doesn't mean they are genuine friendships, but useful when you need information.'

I nod and take a sip of vodka.

'I fired him; it's for the best,' she continues.

'Why?' I ask.

She glares at me. 'I let him use my apartment to work there since his is so small.' She pauses and takes a sip of vodka. 'It was a matter of confidence, and he broke that trust.'

Davian was using her apartment? Why use hers when he has his own? It clicks: the apartment Lottie talked about in Chelsea, that's Giselle's apartment. I rub my forehead. How had Davian allowed himself to be so reckless and stupid? How could he take such a risk? Even if it wasn't for the murder, did he honestly think Giselle wouldn't find out? Took drugs at her office, and had sex in her apartment. He did take her generosity for granted.

'My apartment isn't a hotel where he could bring women to have sex with them,' she says, slamming the glass on the coffee table. 'On my bed, on my sheets. It's disgusting!'

I play with my ear. I don't know what to say. What could I say? In a matter of days, Davian's life had fallen apart. Lottie, the woman he was possibly having an affair with, is dead, he's a suspect in her murder investigation, he got fired from his job, and his reputation is shattered. Melissa might have dumped him as well. I have to talk to him.

How did Lottie know Davian was using Giselle's place in Chelsea to work? Maybe she didn't know. Perhaps she heard it from someone or took a guess.

'Is it true though? Did he have a relationship with Lottie?' I ask.

Giselle spins towards me like a lion ready to attack its prey.

'Don't defend him. Actions have consequences. He should have thought about it before he had sex with a girl who worked for me, who is now murdered. I can't have that kind of attention at the moment. It's bad for business.'

So much for her star photographer.

'Am I fired too? Is that why you came here at this hour?' I ask.

'No, Anthony, you're not fired,' she says, reaching for her bag before making her way out, closing the door firmly behind her.

I take a gulp of vodka. I think of Davian alone in custody accused of Lottie's murder. His life is ruined. I want to see him, speak to him, and get it out of him. Is it all true?

I stand in Chelsea across the street from Giselle's apartment. How many times had Lottie gone in and out with no care in the world? With no regard of what would happen to her? The doors swing open and a woman with flaming red hair and a man come out. DC Gallagher and her partner. I spin around and dash away before they can spot me. Because Davian is in custody, it doesn't mean the investigation is over. I don't glance back as I pace to a trendy café across the road. Did they see me? My heart drums against my chest and my breath is coming out in gasps as if I had been running. I sit by the window.

DC Gallagher and DC Taylor are still outside the apartment. She has her hands on her hips, DC Taylor is gesturing with his hands. She points her finger at him. Boy, she looks pissed off. Are they looking for the laptop?

DC Gallagher stomps away from him and DC Taylor raises his hands up in the air.

I unzip my back bag, take out the laptop, place it on the table and plug in my headphones. I boot the laptop and scan the menu.

***

Lottie's Recordings. Clip Seventeen

I couldn't seem to wipe the smile off my face. I arrived home and looked around. The flat was still empty and then it hit me: I have nothing to grin about. I was alone in the apartment and Davian is not spending Saturday evening with me. I made myself a sandwich and watched TV. 'Is this what my life is going to be like?' I asked myself as I glanced at my half-eaten packet of crisps. Saturdays alone watching TV shows and munching on crisps? What was Davian doing? Is he with her?

Do I enter in his thoughts? Does he smile to himself or go stiff as the afternoon plays in his head? Does he even care? Is this how it's going to be from now onwards? Waiting for him to summon me? Saturdays alone or with Ella or Lilia, when we can be together? I reach for my phone and scroll for his number and I type.

I miss you xxx

Then I delete it. He's not my boyfriend; it gives me no right to miss him or text him. He'd get angry with me for sending it in the first place. There was a knock on the door; every time the bell or the phone rings, I jump, hoping it will be Anthony, but it never is. It was Abdel.

'Forgive me,' he said almost pleadingly. 'I didn't mean to hurt you. I love you. I can't stop thinking about you. Please take me back. I've made a mistake. We can make this work.'

I was paralysed. I tried to speak, but nothing came out. He wrapped his arms around my waist and laid his head on my stomach. He looked so heartbroken and so sad. I felt like shit. Somehow, even though we were not together, I felt I had betrayed him in some way, I cheated on him. I laid my hand on his shoulders.

'Get up,' I said.

My voice sounded firm and steady, unlike how I felt. I'm such a shit; here is a man who loves me, willing to admit he made a mistake, and I couldn't wait to run into Davian's arms.

'Come in,' I said.

***

I unplug my headphones and look at the window. A group of kids walk by, followed by a man in a brown coat, glued to his phone. This is how Abdel came back in the picture, but what about Davian? Did she keep seeing him behind Abdel's back? I rub my jaw, take out a few notes, and place them on the table. I pack the laptop and get up. I walk out of the café, leaving my sandwich untouched. Somehow, listening to all of this, the mess Lottie created in her life made me lose my appetite.

Chapter Twenty-Six

I nip out to buy tea, milk, sugar and bread. I'm walking past the newsagent when a headline in bold stops me in my tracks.

The Secret Life of the Office Girl and Her Killer.

What would her parents think, reading this article about their daughter sleeping with someone who was already in a relationship?

I scan the words *lover, affair, murder*. I didn't buy the newspaper. I didn't want to read about my friends seeing each other behind my back. If only I hadn't acted the way I did at the party, if only I had spoken to her, if only I hadn't gone away, I could have stopped it. I would have stopped Lottie from doing something like this. *No, don't go there*, I think. It wasn't my fault and I wasn't going to blame myself for Lottie's and Davian's actions. I couldn't have stopped her. Or him. It's not like they were going to tell me. How was I supposed to know? It breaks my heart that they, my friends Lottie and Davian, could do this. To end so tragically for both of them. I go back to my flat where nothing awaits me but a laptop. But someone is waiting for me when I return. DC Gallagher is standing by my door. I wonder where DC Taylor is; I thought detectives come in pairs, like socks. She peers at me as I approach. Why a policewoman? When she could have been on the cover of a magazine? I don't see why a policewoman can't look like a Bond girl.

'I was wondering if I can ask you a few more questions,' she says.

'Sure,' I say, and unlock the door.

Of course, she would ask me a few more questions and she'd come back again and again. She isn't going anywhere, not until she gets to the bottom of this.

Good thing I hid the laptop under the bed this morning. DC Gallagher walks in and looks around. The flat has seen better days. There are dirty dishes in the sink, piles of clothes on the sofa. I remove the clothes and the empty mugs from the coffee table. I offer her a drink, but she dismisses it with a wave of her hand. I want to ask her about Davian, but she won't give me any information. She remains on her feet and it makes me uncomfortable.

'Were you aware Davian and Lottie were having an affair?' she asks.

'No, I wasn't,' I reply.

'Davian didn't say anything about this to you?'

'No.'

'Lottie?'

'That's the point of an affair,' I point out.

'Excuse me?'

'An affair is supposed to be kept secret.'

She gives me a look as if to say, 'okay, smart arse'. 'Did Lottie ever say anything to you about being frightened for her life?'

'No.'

'She didn't say anything that made you worry, maybe something in her manner?'

I shake my head. 'No, she didn't.'

'Anthony, you'd better sit down,' she says.

I do as I'm told and DC Gallagher sits down across from me. 'The gun Lottie was shot with, it belonged to her.'

I stare at DC Gallagher, dumbstruck. Lottie had a gun?

Blood drains from my face. 'I don't understand.'

'As one of her closest friends, I was hoping you could shed light on this.'

'She never told me anything about a gun. I mean, it's not something you'd tell people about, would you?'

DC Gallagher keeps her face steady without giving me a response.

'I'm sorry. This is quite a shock,' I say.

'It seems none of you knew Lottie at all,' DC Gallagher says.

I detect a slight irritation in her voice. Did they find Davian's prints on the gun? Is that why he's in custody? I wish I knew.

'We spoke to Ella and she said just about the same thing as you. She was quite surprised when I told her about the gun,' DC Gallagher says, standing.

After DC Gallagher left, I slumped on the sofa; a groan comes out of my mouth and I rub my face with my hands. Lottie was shot with her own gun. Lottie bought a gun. Why? What was she afraid of?

***

Lottie's Recordings. Clip Eighteen

Now that Abdel and I are back together, I'm determined to be good, and the first thing I have to do is explain to Davian I cannot see him anymore. My hands were sweaty and clammy as I paced down the corridor. I see little of Davian, and when I do see him, he's professional but keeps the same tone, as if I am a halfwit. When I knocked on the door, no one answered. I went to ask the receptionist if Davian was around.

'Davian is away,' she told me.

Away where? I wanted to ask her, but I didn't want to expose myself. Was he on holiday with Melissa? Why he didn't tell me? The thought of him lying in bed with her drove me mad. The truth is, after I leave, it's her he goes to, not me. Did he expect that I'd be available to him when he returns? That I'd jump when he leaves me a bloody Post-it? Our meetings were recorded on Post-its. Every time he discards a Post-it, he discards me along with it. Is that what I am to him, a word scribbled on a coloured piece of paper? A reminder or a task? What am I to him?

Meanwhile, Abdel was great. Even though we went to dinners, or he came over with a pizza and we cuddled in front of the TV, Davian lingered there. I thought about him, how good he felt, and his breath on my skin. I snuggled against Abdel as if to stop those thoughts from coming back. We might be back together and this is what I wanted, but something didn't feel right. Not like we were before. Not whole, but broken as if a piece is missing, and we don't quite fit anymore. Beyond repair. It's me, the something we can't repair. I wanted us to get back together back then, not now. I'm convincing myself otherwise.

***

By this time, I had returned from my travels. I felt much more relaxed and ready to face Lottie. Until I heard she and Abdel were back together, so I backed off. I knew Abdel wasn't happy with me, and I didn't want to cause any more rift between them. Now, as I'm watching this clip, it makes me wonder if she dumped Abdel with the hope that Davian would do the same? If that was the case, she built a false pretence and it was a foolish act.

***

When Davian returned, I was anxious. I kept walking to his studio, staring at the closed door and changing my mind. I did this back and forth until Giselle marched through the corridor and I ran away. I went on with my day, with photocopying, assisting an artist with her exhibition. I returned to my cubical and a Post-it was waiting for me. I snatched the paper and stomped to his studio.

I have never been in his studio before, and his icy glare told me I was unwelcome. This was his space.

It seemed too detached from everything as if I'd stepped into an empty world.

'Did you miss me that much that you couldn't wait to see me?' he said with a raised eyebrow.

His tone sounded sarcastic, mocking even.

I handed him the note.

'I can't do this,' I said, surprised how confident I sounded while my body twitched.

He broke eye contact. 'This again? I don't have time for this-'

'Abdel and I are back together,' I announced.

'Oh.' His blue eyes went to me, then glanced down at the table. 'What about me?'

Him? What about him? The last time I checked, he was still in a relationship. He went on a trip with her doing God knows what and he has the nerve to ask me this? It was so selfish and condescending.

'What about you?' I said, raising an eyebrow at him.' You're still with Melissa, aren't you?'

'I meant us?' he said.

'There is no us, Davian, and there never will be. I can't sit around and wait for you to put a ridiculous Post-it on my desk. I won't settle for second best! Is this what I am to you? A Post-it? I want more and you can't give me that. I'm going to hand in my letter of resignation to Giselle in a few days.'

'We'll talk later, okay?' he said, giving me a hard-stern look.

Did he hear a word I just said? The nerve of this guy.

'There won't be a later,' I said, walking to the door.

***

She didn't quit, however, or never got the chance to do it. I don't know. I go for a walk. I have no idea where I am, but my feet keep taking me forward with Lottie and Davian's words reverberating in my mind, each piece of truth, each lie that had been told. What did he want from her? Was it his mission to torment her? That prick. Tiny droplets form a pattern on the pavement. A clap of thunder crashes in the distance. I look up at the grey sky with its low clouds. I turn and stroll all the way back.

Ella is waiting on the step, her head darting to each person who walks by. She seems rather agitated.

'Ella?' I say.

'Oh,' she says, standing up and dusting herself off. 'I didn't recognise you there.'

'Yeah, well,' I say, removing the hoodie off my head. 'You been waiting long?'

'About half an hour.'

'Why didn't you text?'

She waves her phone. 'Battery died.'

'Ah…'

'Do you have a moment? I need to talk to you.'

'Sure. You can charge your phone when we're in,' I say, putting the key in the door.

I unlock the door and wait for her to go in. The laptop is on the kitchen table. I grab it and take it to the bedroom.

'Can you put the kettle on?' I shout.

'Yeah!' she says.

I open the closet and place the laptop with a pile of clothes. I hear Ella moving about, flicking a lighter, humming to herself. When I emerge in the kitchen, she's leaning by the counter, smoking. I bet she has many questions. Questions I cannot answer for her.

'So, it is true? The police were right; there was a man,' she says.

'It seems like it.'

'And is Davian that man?' she said with distaste in her voice.

'It could be him.'

She frowns. 'I don't know why she kept it from us.'

The kettle boils. 'There is a reason why she kept it from us.'

Ella shrugs and turns her back to me and starts to help herself with the mugs and tea. 'Because he has a girlfriend.'

'Yes.'

'It's odd, I didn't think he would... I mean, the way she spoke about him. He treated her as if she were invisible. It's hard to believe after that she... he...' Ella pauses and places the mug in front of me. 'I'm hurt. I'm hurt she would do something like this. I know she had a crush on him, but to go and do what she did...'

She sits across from me and we smoke quietly. There is a look of bewilderment on Ella's face.

'Him? Really? Does she know? The girlfriend, I mean?'

Davian's words echo in my mind. Lottie was a pathological liar.

'I don't know.'

'Still him.' Ella says, turning the mug so the ear is facing her. 'Lottie was beautiful and kind.'

She was beautiful and kind? If Lottie were kind, she wouldn't leave this laptop, this burden. She wouldn't sleep with a man who had someone else. I can't shake the feeling she lent me this laptop for a reason. I think she wanted me to see these videos, that somehow, she planned this. Why?

'I'm sure that her beauty had nothing to do with it, there were plenty of stunning women who were willing to share Davian's bed, and he never paid any attention. He didn't associate himself with unconnected females,' I say, mashing the cigarette in the ashtray.

Her eyes dart to me. 'And she was connected to you?'

'Yes. I'm getting the impression that he...' I trail off.

She tips her teabag. 'He?'

'It's nothing.'

'Anthony!'

'He did it to hurt me,' I confess.

Her jaw drops. 'But he's your best friend? Friends don't do that to each other.'

I shake my head. 'We are... I mean, we were close, but in time, we drifted apart.'

'Why?'

'Didn't you have friends that you were close with and then you stop hearing from them or meeting them?' I say, lighting another cigarette.

She thinks for a moment. 'Sometimes.'

'It kind of happened with Davian. He had Melissa and he was constantly travelling and he's a bit of a hermit.'

'A hermit who was having an affair with our friend,' Ella points out. 'That explains why she left Abdel.'

'In those months when she broke up with Abdel throughout... her last days, did you notice any difference in her behaviour at all?' I ask.

'No, not really.'

'He denies it though,' I say. 'The affair.'

'Of course, he'll deny it.'

'No, but...'

Ella scowls at me. 'Don't tell me you believe him.'

'I don't know who to believe,' I grumbled.

'The police came to talk to me again,' Ella says.

'They came to speak to me too.'

'Did they ask you if Lottie owned a laptop?'

This hangs in the air, but I hold her gaze. *Careful, I think to myself, one false move and she'll know I'm up to something.* 'No, not about the laptop. But they told me Lottie bought a gun registered under her name.'

'Yes, they told me that too. I mean Lottie buying a gun? She must have been afraid of something.'

'She never told you anything about a gun?' I ask.

Ella shakes her head.

'Why did they question you about the laptop? Wasn't it at her apartment?' I ask, keeping my voice cool.

'Apparently not. They wouldn't ask about it if they'd found it.'

I shift on my seat. That could be why DC Gallagher was so pissed with DC Taylor; they must be looking for it. They are looking for it for a reason. I have to be careful. I can't be seen in public with it. What if they are tracking my moves? What if they get the CCTV? The city is crawling with them. How can I be so careless? I think of the places I had been with it. Shit.

'I can't believe she had been so secretive, about Davian, the gun and everything else.'

I want to tell her that the laptop is here, in my closet. That it has videos Lottie had recorded in the last year of her life. I want to go down on my knees and beg her not to tell the police, but I can't do that. Nothing will stop Ella from going to the police. So I sit there and lie to her face just like Lottie and Davian did.

Ella runs her hand through her hair. 'I miss her.'

'I miss her too.'

Ella sips her tea. 'How are you holding up?'

'It's hard, but I have to let go eventually. Life goes on.'

What did the police find on her phone? The last call she made, the last message she sent or received? Were there any messages from Davian? It seemed they only communicated through letters and Posts-its. What about what her mother said? That she saw Davian and Lottie arguing outside the house? How did Davian get in touch with her if he wasn't texting Lottie? Not by a Post-it, that's for sure, and I checked her emails and there was nothing from him. He must have got in touch with her somehow and Lottie had his number. Lottie said she attempted to send him a text him then deleted it. Davian went to great lengths to cover up their shags.

'Are you in there, Anthony?'

Ella's voice brings me back to reality.

'I'm sorry, what?'

She's smiling now. 'You were miles away.'

'Sorry, I...' I trail off.

She stands. 'I'd better be going.'

I walk her to the door. I don't know what happened next. Maybe I pulled her back in, or she came back in but the door is closed and Ella is back inside, leaning against the wall. My hands are riding up her skirt as if I'm hunting for treasure, her lips are on mine, and she moans softly. The clothes come off. I pick her up and carry her to the bedroom.

Chapter Twenty-Seven

I try not to think about what just happened. I don't think Ella wants to discuss it either. We're two people caught in a terrible storm in our lives. This is our pain, our grief. This is ours to carry. We are the ones who understand each other. Even though we are friends and we never saw each other that way, we'll do anything to make the pain go away, even for a few minutes. Maybe she had thought about it; that's why she came here with the perfect excuse of the police looking for the laptop. Lottie and Ella are friends and I swim between them, those women all linked to me. I glance at the closet, where the laptop rests with its secrets. My burden.

We both get dressed in silence and again I walk her to the door and open it for her. She turns and strokes my cheek, her eyes studying my face as if we're never going to see each other again. Maybe we won't; it's not the right time to see if I can fit her into my timetable.

'Don't worry about it,' she says, kissing me on the lips. 'I wanted it too.'

So it was in her mind.

'Thanks,' she said.

***

Lottie's Recordings. Clip Nineteen

On Monday, I woke up with a sense of dread. On my way to the office I bought a croissant as I always do, and ate it while walking there. Giselle was already in her office. She smiled and said, 'I thought you were not coming in today?'

'Was I not?' I said, dumbfounded. 'No, I think you got me confused with someone else.'

'Davian told me you were going to help him out.'

My heart sank; he can't just go to Giselle and tell her that I am not coming in, and help him with what?

'Speak of the devil,' Giselle said.

I glanced at Giselle; couldn't she see it on my face that I didn't want to be alone with this man? He was crazy and unpredictable and he is going to make me change my mind. I wanted to scream.

'I'll take it from here,' Davian said.

Giselle's eyes went to Davian, then to me. I wondered if she could tell that something was going on. When she closed the door, I turned to him.

'What do you think you're doing?' I hissed at him.

'Stopping you from making a big mistake.'

'Mistake!'

I sighed and plodded to the corridor. Lilia walked by.

'Are you okay?' she asked.

'I'm fine,' I said.

Davian was behind me telling Lilia 'good morning' as I felt her eyes burning on my back. I wonder if she suspects too. We rode the lift side by side.

'What do you think you're doing? Going to Giselle telling her I'll be working with you today?'

'You are going to work with me today. There is something I have to show you.'

'You can't just decide-'

'You'll see,' he said.

***

This video is the longest, over an hour long. I make myself a cup of tea and look out the window, watching a woman pushing a stroller and my neighbour watering the plants. It comes crashing down so hard that it makes my body spasm. I sit on the floor. I cry for Lottie, for Davian, for them both. For their betrayal. I cry for Davian being in custody for her murder. I cry for my pain, for the loss of my two friends, friends I didn't know at all. I cry for the hurt I'm feeling and for not trusting me enough to tell me all of this. Is she seeing me right now from whatever place she is in? Is she laughing at me? Does she feel sorry for what she did? Is there any remorse? Does she look back with regret? Did she think about her parents? How heartbroken they are right now? Of all the men she could be with, she chose the one who was the least unattainable? The more out of reach Davian was, the more his manipulation furthered, the more she desired him, the more control it gave him. It gave him power without her even knowing. Lottie is a pathological liar, he said. How was she a liar exactly? If she was making stuff up about him, how come no one knows anything about it?

Chapter Twenty-Eight

Davian has been released on bail. It has been on the news.

Suspected Killer Released.

I focus on the headline. What happened to innocent until proven guilty? If he's released, it must be because the police don't have enough evidence to charge Davian with. I call him, but my call goes straight to voicemail.

We all have that moment when for an instant, for a fraction of a second, our heart stops, and we hold our breath as we see the most beautiful thing we have ever seen. We stare for as long as we can; we might be brave enough to approach, but then we move on.

***

Lottie's Recordings. Clip Nineteen-continued

I followed him to the parking lot. He took out a key, pressed a switch and a black Ford Fiesta beeped. In the car, the radio was on, filling the empty silence between us. It was a silly thought, but I felt as if he was going to take me away from all the city's nonsense and transport me into a new world. Where was he taking me? I started to doze on and off, opening my eyes to see where we were going until the familiarity was gone. I didn't recognise the streets anymore. The Smiths were playing as he drove with one hand on the wheel, the other resting on his head, deep in thought. We drove into Croydon. He stopped the car in a narrow road, then smiled and told me we have arrived.

'Where?' I asked, flummoxed.

He took a bag with him containing his camera. I trailed after him. He opened his bag and took out an expensive-looking camera. I watched with fascination as he took a couple of shots. I glance up to see what he was shooting and my mouth drops. It is one of the saddest sights I have ever seen. Nothing could explain why, from all the locations he could photograph, he chose this particular joint. It was a house, a large one made of red bricks. Once it belonged to someone, a home that was loved and cherished. I pictured a couple living there with their children and a dog. Funny how the brain works; when we picture a couple, we picture them with two perfect children and a dog. The shutter of the camera sang in my ears, all those Christmases, birthdays, and anniversaries spent in this house.

Click.

All that was left were the echoes of this family: a faded photograph. What it stood for or what was left of it was a sad and lonely demolished house.

Click.

It was beyond repair; part of the front wall of the second floor had fallen away, and a pile of bricks stood like a tiny mountain on the ground.

Click.

Part of the roof was destroyed; this house must have been vacant for years.

Click.

The windows were broken.

Click.

It stood there begging and crying for someone to love it again, to become a home, to serve as a barrier of safety and protection, not obsolete, worn down, inhabited.

Click.

Click.

Click.

'Can you turn the sound off?' I asked.

Davian had a strange look upon his face.

'Sure,' he said, making his way to the house.

'Where are you going?' I asked, the panic rising in my voice.

He looked back at me. 'In.'

'But...' I stared up at the house that now has grown bigger, 'it's dangerous,' I said.

'Come, it will be fine.'

He held his hand as if he were a prince leading me to his castle.

I surveyed the house once more, a chill running down my spine that had nothing to do with the cold. He led the way. The front door was off by its hinges and lay broken on the pavement. I covered my nose with my hand. The house smelt of boiled eggs combined with an overpowering smell of decay and burned wood. I felt the croissant making its way up and I tried to prevent myself from being sick. There were old newspapers, torn pages from magazines and old books scattered all over the wooden floors. There was a chair without a seat, a large hole in a wall. A fireplace, a real one. One side of a wall was black. This house was devastated; someone set it on fire. I felt ill.

'Why have you brought me here?'

He was going up the stairs.

'Davian!' I yelled.

He stopped and sighed. 'Come up, I'll explain.'

The wood creaked under my shoes as I climbed the stairs. There were more books and old newspapers. He stood by the wall taking pictures. Why this house?

'Don't go in the middle,' he warned. 'The floors are not safe.'

'I want to go home,' I cried.

He looked at me tenderly. 'This house is going to be taken down soon. That's why I'm taking photos of it.'

'Not for the sake of art?' I ask.

He looks down at his shoes. 'No.' His eyes flew to me. 'Go to the edge.'

'What?'

'Go to the edge. I want to take a picture of you walking over there.'

***

Where is this house, anyway, in Croydon? She filmed this a year ago; the house might have been taken down by now. What if this house is another hoax? If it's true, if they did go to the house and

Davian had taken pictures of it, wouldn't he have copies? How could I ask him about it without exposing myself?

Chapter Twenty-Nine

I ring the bell at Davian's apartment. No answer. I try again. I tap my feet on the pavement; maybe he's at his parents. Why haven't I thought about it before? As I'm about to turn and leave, the buzzer goes off. Davian's immaculate appearance has dissolved into one of unwashed messed-up hair, dark circles under his eyes and blemished skin. He looks like shit, but these past few weeks haven't been easy on him, and it shows.

'Good for you to come,' he said.

'It's not a problem. This what friends are for.'

He shrugs as he sits on the sofa and puts a cigarette in his mouth. He offers me the packet. I take it and light a cigarette myself. We smoke in silence.

'So, you're out,' I said.

'Yeah, for the time being,' he says, not looking at me.

'Oh.'

'They found something that might change the course of the case,' he says.

'What?' I ask.

I get a glare as a reply. He stands and paces the room.

'The bitch set me up.'

'Who? Lottie?'

He stops pacing. 'Yeah, they found my clothes in her apartment.'

'Well... were you at her apartment?'

'I don't even know where she lived!'

I stand. 'Okay, calm down.'

He sinks down on the floor, grabbing bits of his dirty hair.

'She stole them and placed them there,' he says.

I blink at him. 'How could she?'

He breaks eye contact.

'Davian, did you or didn't you have an affair with Lottie?'

He glances up at me, his small blue eyes watering. I wait, trying to be calm although it seems impossible. I look for traces of Melissa, but there are none. She's gone. Davian is alone. No one believes him. He's on his own. But he's not. I'll be there for him.

'I don't know why women like me. I told you this before, for the life of me, I don't know. I had girls writing me love letters, which made their way to the bin, girls throwing themselves at me. I dismissed them all, but I never encountered anyone as persistent as Lottie.' He looks up at me with puppy dog eyes. 'She was obsessed. I think she took my clothes from my office.'

He's avoiding the question.

'The police found two of my ties at the apartment and a shirt.'

'You still haven't answered my question; did you sleep with her?'

I get another icy cold glare. 'No, I didn't. She was making up stuff about me.'

'But Giselle said you took Lottie to her apartment in Chelsea.'

'I didn't. The police looked on the CCTV and they never found any footage of Lottie going in the apartment.'

He stands. His shoulders relax a little.

'You have no idea what I have been through these past few days; I had everything I needed, a job, a girlfriend, and my reputation intact. Now, I have nothing. I turned Lottie down repeatedly. She wouldn't take no for an answer. So she started spreading lies, but I never thought it would amount to this.'

What about the photograph he gave her and the Post-its? Lottie had recorded clips, giving explicit details of her relationship with him while Davian says he never laid a finger on her. Who is lying? Lottie? Davian? What did the police find to release Davian? No solid evidence to charge him?

'She was shot!' I shout. 'How could she possibly have been setting you up?'

He lowers his head. 'I don't know, but something is not right. Now, if you don't mind, I'd like to be alone.'

I stare at him.

'Please?' he begs.

I nod and turn to take my leave.

I don't know what's going on. Davian says one thing and Lottie's clips say another. How did she know so much if it wasn't true? She had one hell of an imagination to make all of this up. What about the house she talks about on the video? How did she know about that if it weren't true? I'm sure there are people who saw them together or argue. How had Davian concealed everything from everyone, including Giselle? I'm sure if he told her what Lottie was doing, Giselle would have taken action. Why had he hid it? Was he embarrassed? Because of Melissa finding out and not believing him? I go back to the flat, where the laptop waits for me with either Lottie's truth or her lies.

***

Lottie's Recordings. Clip Nineteen- continued

Why did he want to take a photo of me walking to the edge? God this was so strange, I thought.

'Nobody is going to know it's you, don't worry,' he said.

I kept staring at him.

'Go on,' he urged.

It was easy for him to say. What if I fall to my death? I turned and looked at the open space that once was a wall; now all I can see is the fence and the large building behind it. I took tiny steps and the wood wailed under me and my heart thumped against my chest. I took another step looking down at my shoes. I stopped walking.

'A bit further,' Davian instructed.

'God, stop being so odd!'

No reply came.

My muscles tightened.

Click.

Click.

Click.

I shut my eyes as I made it to the edge only a few inches away. If I make the wrong move, I fall.

I heard sounds of another world, not part of this one. Birds, cars, and horns.

'God damn it, Davian. I'm scared of fucking heights!' I shouted.

I turned around, being careful with my footing. Davian stood behind me.

What he said next, it was so out of the blue, that I didn't know if I should laugh or cry.

'Leave him,' he said. 'I'll leave Melissa and we'll be together, and I'll give you more.'

***

I press pause and rub my mouth. I sigh, not knowing whom to believe. I have this laptop and Davian insists he never had any intimate relationship with Lottie. Then why go to the trouble? Who killed Lottie?

***

My eyes bulged. He can't be serious. Was he suggesting we leave our partners to be together, break their hearts? He had to be joking.

'You want me to leave Abdel for you?' I asked.

'Why not? You think it will work?'

'I don't know, I hardly think I'm your type.'

'You don't know what my type is.'

Every time I glanced down, my stomach lurched and my head started to hurt. My eyes went up to him, so very beautiful, it took my breath away and he was offering himself to me. He could be mine. For a moment, a thought crept in: he was so close, there was no distance between us. Would he push me? Would he do it and be rid of me?

'You would really leave her to be with me?' I ask, my hand curling on his shirt. His hand was on my lower back.

'Yes, I will. I think. We'll be very happy.'

'Do you think so?'

'Oh yes,' he said, and kissed me so passionately, it turned my bones into water.

***

What did they do next according to her? Have sex surrounded by all that havoc and melancholy?

It crawls up at me; the acid rises up from my stomach. I rush to the bathroom and vomit. I hadn't eaten anything for the whole day so, there wasn't much in my system. I spit the bile. I stand and crane my head under the sink, washing away the foul taste in my mouth, and then slump on the sofa, rubbing my head.

***

My hand found its way to his groin, feeling his stiffness. We made love surrounded by all that depression and ugliness.

In the car, we were silent as he drove out of Croydon. Davian smoked, his eyes on the road. I looked at the trees and the gloomy grey sky; it was about to rain soon. Can I do it? Leave Abdel so we can be together at last? This is what I want, so why do I feel so hesitant? Why is there that feeling in the pit of my stomach? An uncertainty. There was a tiny voice whispering, "Don't do it."

I wanted to discuss it more deeply. I glanced at him, at this beautiful man who a few moments ago, I'd had my legs wrapped around, while we looked at each other with such rapt attention as we filled each other with passion. Now, there is distance again and I'm afraid to talk to him. That's not normal if we are to embark on a relationship. I have to feel comfortable around him.

How am I going to break this to Abdel? I wanted him to come back and he did. I can't hurt him, although he did hurt me. I'm not going to tell him the truth, but I have to do this somehow. I sat there in the car with the radio playing pop songs as I fantasised what my life with Davian would be like. We would snuggle and cuddle, then that illusion was shattered with another thought. This will come out in the open and everyone will know. Ella, Lilia, Giselle, all the people in the office, and all the women who fancy him. They will rip me apart with just their glances. How did she manage to do it? They would think why her? What does she have that I don't? Then another wave of emotion crept into me as I thought of Anthony. I haven't heard from him for months; are we still even friends? Somehow, I didn't care what my friends and co-

workers thought, but what Anthony has to say. That sure as hell bothers me.

***

I jump up the sofa.

'Arsehole!' I roar at the laptop. 'Why are you doing this? You're just a machine programmed with software and created by mankind. Why do you have to contain such devastating details?'

I snatch the bottle of vodka and take a gulp. I glare at the arsehole laptop, with its arsehole information, and the biggest arsehole of them all is her. Not Davian, but Lottie. Her stupidity goes beyond any comprehension. She's a fucking disgrace. I sit in front of the arsehole laptop and fire up a cigarette.

***

I've done it! I was sitting on the chair in the kitchen when Abdel walked in with purchases from the supermarket. We planned to cook together that evening.

'You look gloomy. What's wrong?' he asked.

'You should go.'

He searched my face quizzically; at first, he thought I was kidding.

'Go where?' he asked smiling.

'Out of my life.'

His mouth dropped. 'What?'

'You heard me. It's over. I don't want to be with you anymore. I can't do this. It's not going to work.'

'Wait, wait, wait, are you serious?'

I glared at him.

He stood there, rubbing his face in confusion. 'I thought we...'

I walked past him. 'I've changed my mind.'

'You've changed your mind or you're fucking someone else?' he yelled.

I turn my back to him so he won't see my tears.

'It's over, go. Disappear.'

'I'm not leaving until you tell me what I have done wrong!'

'You've done nothing wrong. It's me.'

'Bullshit. There is a reason. I want to know. I have every right to know.'

I wiped my tears away and took the ashtray from the table.

'Goodbye, Abdel.'

I stomped to the bedroom and shut the door.

I stood in the middle of the room, holding my stomach as if I were in great pain. I heard him move about, throwing something against the wall; heavy footsteps cross the hall and a slam of the door that makes the flat shake.

Chapter Thirty

Her expression in this clip is serious. She pushes her long waves away from her face and her eyes fall to the floor. I place the mug on the table. There is shaking then, a crashing sound as the screen slides sideways. All I can see are her bare feet. There is a long silence. I jump when she screams, almost inhuman.

***

Lottie's Recordings. Clip Twenty

'I can't believe I fucked up my life to make a total fool of myself!' she roared.

***

A vase drops on the floor by her feet. I stare at the screen in horror. This woman wasn't Lottie; she's not the sweet, good-natured girl I once knew. This is someone else, a demon possessed who looked like Lottie.

***

'I knew it was too good to be true. Why wouldn't he be with me? That son of a bitch tricked me!'

***

She paced up and down, stepping on the broken glass. My face goes white. Why didn't she reach out to anyone? Blood is dripping off her feet; it leaves bloody footprints as she paces in front of the laptop and keeps stepping on the glass, pressing her feet on purpose.

***

He needs more time. The fucking twat, you know, what he told me because I say you jump, you go and do it? Miserable git! I scared Lilia when she found me crying in the bathroom this afternoon. If I'd told her, she would give me the answer that I didn't want to hear. I will get him where it hurts. I'll show him I'm not someone to be fucked with.

***

Show him? What the hell did she do? By now her obsession had exacerbated. If she didn't have Davian, she'd find ways to fuck him over. The more I find out, the more disturbed I become. I lie in the dark smoking, hoping sleep will come. My body is resting but my brain refuses to shut off. Sleeping hurts, but I'm tired. So I lie in bed, waiting for sleep and creating scenarios in my head. What if I show Davian these clips and he sees her ghost emerging from the laptop to haunt him? He'd be terrified. He'll insist she's a liar. Would she get into this trouble to create fiction? No, they're both liars. I have to get to the bottom of this and find the truth.

When Lottie and I reconciled, it didn't look like something was wrong, that she was harassing

Davian as he put it, or she was having a passionate affair with him as she's stating.

'What have you been up to?' I asked her after I told her where I had been and the places I had seen.

'Oh, nothing much. Abdel and I are over again.'

'Why?'

'Oh, life,' she said. 'He's not someone I want to be with.'

'Not someone you want to be with?' I asked her. 'And who you want to be with?'

She looked at me then. 'I see myself with someone who's passionate and in control.'

Someone passionate and in control. Someone like Davian. Was it here that she was planning to bring him down? Why would Lottie want to own a gun? I didn't think she would waltz into a gun shop and buy one. Where did she get it from? I'd very much like to know.

Another thing that bothered me was Lottie didn't give a shit about Melissa. To her, Melissa was the enemy; she had no regard for her feelings. How would Lottie have felt if someone did the same to her? Someone who took her man and didn't give a flying fuck about her feelings.

The more unreachable and unavailable Davian was, the more her desire expanded. Lottie thought Davian had this exciting life; she would have been disappointed. He hardly went out. He locked himself in his flat and buried himself in work. He went out for an exhibition; if he could, he would avoid that as well. She wanted him with all of her might. Lottie would have lied and cheated; to have him was all that mattered. She treated the situation as if Davian were a beautiful and exotic accessory. Her love was unrequited. Davian loved another and Lottie couldn't stand it. She was too demanding and clingy to give him the space he sought. That neediness was what would put him off in the first place.

Chapter Thirty-One

The sound of the buzzer explodes in the room. I go to the window to check who it is. Davian. I unplug the laptop and place it inside my backpack. As I turn, the bag falls on the floor and my heart stops. The last thing I need is to break the laptop when I've made it this far. I pick up the bag and the photograph Davian had given to Lottie drops to my feet. I pick it up and flip it over. The buzzer makes me jump. I shove the photo in the bag along with the laptop.

Davian looks better. His eyes are still red and puffy, though the hair is back to its former glory.

'I was about to make a cup of tea. Would you like one?' I ask.

'Coffee,' he says.

I go to the kitchen and fill a kettle of water. Davian sits on the kitchen table and lights a cigarette.

'Melissa came.'

'She did?'

'Yes, for her stuff. She left. For good.'

'I'm sorry.'

'Yeah. Me too.'

'Have you heard anything else from the police?'

He stares into space as if he's thinking about something.

'Not yet. You know what DC Gallagher told my lawyer? The way the gun was positioned on the floor, how it was found, the shot was from a close range. Still, something doesn't add up.'

'She told that to your lawyer?'

'She did.'

'Why would she?'

'I don't know, but apparently, they found marks on the furniture in Lottie's apartment.'

'Is your lawyer sleeping with the policewoman?'

Davian smiled.

I made a cup of tea for me and black coffee with two sugars for him.

'There is something I have to tell you.'

I placed the mugs on the table. I search his face, but he gives nothing away.

'I haven't been completely honest with you and I should have,' Davian begins.

The silence stretches and lingers in the room while I sit there with aching muscles, waiting for him.

'It's about Lottie.'

I swallow my dread. 'What about her?'

He lowers his head and takes a deep drag from his cigarette to buy himself time. He casts me a look full of sorrow and despair and that's when I know. Lottie wasn't lying. She wasn't making stuff up. He's the liar.

'You son of a bitch,' I hiss, my fists smashing down hard on the table. 'You lying, cold, vindictive son of a bitch!'

Davian raises his hand. 'Let me explain.'

I knock the mug over and it flies straight on the floor.

'Anthony,' Davian says.

His voice is calm, but I can detect something else: worry.

'Explain!' I shout from the top of my lungs.

Davian is on his feet and there is a moment of silence before he slumps down on the chair.

'That night of my exhibition a year ago, after the party, Lottie came to pick up a fight. Giselle was there and she took us to the office, to this vacant room. We argued, things got heated then she started crying and… and…'

At least his side of the story agrees with hers.

'You had sex with her?'

He hesitates. 'Yes… I regretted it right away. I don't know what got into me, she was there, crying. She was wearing this dress and she looked beautiful. I wanted her to stop crying. I wanted to comfort her and…' He pauses, takes a sip of coffee. I take a deep breath. He did comfort her all right, and sank himself further into a bottomless hole.

'I confronted her a few days after. I took her out for dinner to explain it couldn't happen again,' Davian added.

Davian fired a cigarette and tilted his head back as he inhaled, watching the smoke dance in the air.

'And started an affair?' I asked.

'No, I didn't. I wasn't interested. I felt bad enough for what I did, let alone start an affair. Lottie didn't take it very well. She thought we would end up together or something. She left the restaurant.'

My brain ticks like a bomb about to explode but in the clip, she said… Was it all a lie?

'I tried to avoid going to the office as much as I could. When I did go, I stayed in my office. But each time I left, she was there lingering.'

'So, you're saying after you had sex with her, she started making stuff up about you?'

'Anthony, I know she was your friend and this is a delicate matter. I didn't mean to... have sex with her. It was all too intense,' he says with a slight tremor in his voice. 'It's like she wanted... me, but not me.' He puffs on the cigarette. 'I don't know how to explain it... she had this idea in her head. An idea of her and me.'

'Did Melissa know?'

'Of course, Melissa didn't know,' he said, incredulous.

'So, Lottie threatened you. She'd tell Melissa if you didn't accept her... advances?'

'That came later.'

'Later?'

'It was twisted.'

If he lied to me about having sex with her, he could be lying to me now. Davian isn't the most reliable of sources by the looks of it.

'She was playing this sick game with me. A game I wanted no part of. She couldn't take a hint.'

'Davian, be frank with me. Giselle told me you were bringing Lottie to her apartment for sex. Is it true?'

'No, I told you it's not true. That's bullshit; the police checked all CCTV. They questioned the doormen who work there. There is no record of her ever being there. Lottie has never been in that apartment. Who do you think I am, anyway?'

I paced down the room. 'At the moment? I don't know.'

How did Lottie find out Giselle let Davian use one of her apartments? Did she follow him? In her clips, she sounded convincing. How she described the interior of the hallway and the apartment. The whole dialogue, all of it sounds real.

'Giselle asked her to help me with a photoshoot I was doing in a house in Croydon. It's an abandoned thing. I found it by accident and wanted to capture it. I suspect that Lottie told her something. I tried to explain to Giselle that I didn't need Lottie with me and I knew what I was doing.'

'So you never told Giselle what Lottie was doing to you because you feared Melissa would find out?' I reasoned.

'Pretty much.'

'Giselle was your boss. She would have handled the situation with decorum. It's not like she was going to gossip about it,' I pointed out. 'I'm sure she would have dealt with it.'

'I thought I could handle it. What sort of man would I be if I went hiding behind my boss's skirt?'

Of course, his ego got the best of him. Look where it got him now: a suspect in a murder case, and his life is practically ruined.

'Besides, it would be embarrassing exposing myself like that. It's not like I was innocent, given I was the one who seduced Lottie.'

'What happened then?'

'I confronted Lottie and told her to stop what she was doing. What happened between us was a mistake and to accept it.'

'But you went to the house with her?'

'Well, I didn't have much of a choice in the matter since Giselle said so.'

'You could have said no. I mean, you were Giselle's star. She would have taken your side.'

He glares at me.

'So you took her to the house, then what?'

'I took pictures. She watched.'

Was it true? Did he take a picture of her? I can't ask because he would ask me how I would know and I would be exposing myself. I wasn't going to tell him I had a possession of Lottie's, a very important one. Crucial to the case.

'So that's all you did, took the pictures? You have copies to prove that you did go to this house?'

'Yes, I do. The police have them. They might be in an evidence bag at the police station.'

'And went back to the office?' I say.

There was a long silence. He lowers his head, his Adam's apple bobbing up and down.

It was all clear what it meant.

'You idiot! She was infatuated by you; you wouldn't have sex with her again. My God, Davian, you were leading her on.'

His eyes start to water. 'I thought if I gave her what she wanted, she'd leave me alone.'

Lottie was telling half-truths. All the parts of the apartment were made up, at least that's what Davian is saying, but the part about the house is true. The memory flashed before my eyes, how Davian and I had met. It was in secondary school. He was the shy boy, always sitting in the back scribbling in his notebook. I too sat in the back, not paying attention to the lesson. I used to fall asleep or draw. One afternoon, I saw about four boys from my class whose names I can't remember ganging up on Davian. One of them took the notebook from his hand, began tearing out pages, and threw it across the yard. I couldn't sit by and watch; I had to do something. I walked up to them.

'Four against one, seriously?' I said.

'Shut up,' one of them said.

I told them to take a walk. One of them pointed his finger in my face and said it wasn't over. I collected Davian's notebook; there were drawings and good ones. He didn't look me straight in the eye. I told him to stick with me and we'd never looked back since.

'Did you tell the police what you just told me?' I asked, returning to the present.

'I have.'

'And?'

'There isn't enough evidence to charge me with her murder.'

'What if they do find evidence to charge you?'

Now he looks afraid. 'I don't know what she was doing, but Lottie held grudges, or at least with me she did because I didn't... want her.'

'You should have thought about that before you had sex with her... twice,' I pointed out sourly.

Lottie is brought back to life, sitting with us. As all of this unfolds, how she played us all, made us look like fools. Her plan has worked; she wanted to hurt Davian and now she has. She continues to haunt us from her grave. I can almost see her with her long brown hair, wearing that innocent expression on her face. Lottie wasn't as innocent as I thought. She caught us in her web. Me, what was I to her? Friend, companion, a shoulder to cry on, ally, fool? Davian: obsession, lover, tormenter.

'Emily, Lottie's mother, told me she saw you outside her house. What were you doing there?'

'I went to confront Lottie to leave me the fuck alone. She kept telling me I couldn't use her and throw her away.'

'In her defence, you did use her and throw her away,' I said dryly.

He sighs and rubs his temples. 'I'm aware I made a mistake. Twice... Lottie wanted me-'

'She wanted you to leave Melissa to be with her, is that it?' I said, cutting him off.

'And when she realized I wasn't going to do that, she got murdered.'

He sounds like someone who had a motive to have her killed. She wanted him to leave the safety with Melissa to be with her.

'Davian, I'm going to be very frank here. Are you sorry she's dead?' I ask.

The question is crude, but given Davian's questionable morals, I had to ask.

Davian's eyes go wide. 'Of course, I'm sorry she's dead.'

He stood to leave and I walked him to the door.

'This is a lot to take in,' I said.

'I should have told you from the start; I should have told you as soon as...'

'Davian, can I ask you a question?'

'Do you have to ask?'

'During the time when you were a bit... hard on her... did you give her a photograph with a neon heart?'

He stares at me blankly. 'Yes, I did.'

I thought he would ask me how I knew but he didn't. Either he presumed Lottie might have told me, or he had too much on his plate to ask me about it. After Davian left, I took out the photo from my bag and turned it over as if I would find something. There is nothing written there.

***

Lottie's Recordings. Clip Twenty-One

I had to go and find out myself. I saw what I needed to see. Now, I know that it was all a fantasy; I couldn't believe I left a man who loved me for this! I can't take it anymore, him jerking me around. I had to see it to believe it. I did the unthinkable. I could have been fired if I were caught. I didn't tell anyone, not even Lilia. I kept my workload so I could stay behind when everyone left and I made sure Giselle wasn't there either. I went to her office. Her laptop was password protected, but I didn't need it. I went to her filing cabinet instead, where she kept her staff records. I had to make sure; I didn't want it to be true. I found his file and his address was in Westminster, not Chelsea. Then to whom did that apartment belong? What else was he lying to me about? I knew it! God, I can't believe I had been so foolish and gullible.

The next morning, I borrowed my mum's car and I found the apartment in Westminster. I waited three hours until Davian came out with her. I got out of the car and stood far enough away so he wouldn't see me. He was holding her hand, smiling and giggling like a pair of teenagers. The way he looked at her, full of compassion, kissing her forehead; he never did that with me, and never will. He loved her, not me. He isn't going to leave her and has no intention of doing so. He was giving me false hopes and wasting my time. I left Abdel for him. I have given him my body. He went as far as showing up at my parents' house when I stayed over the weekend. My mum had seen me with him and was asking too many questions. This is too much. Did Davian actually think that he could treat me this way and get away with it? I will not be defeated by a bad man who will not love me back. He made me shit all over my relationship, now I'll shit all over his. I drove out there sobbing. I hate her! What does she have that I don't? I despise her. I want to hurt her. I fucking hate her. But the person I hate the most is Davian. I want to hurt him the most.

***

I can think of endless reasons why Lottie hated Melissa with every fibre of her being, cursing her very existence. Lottie hated Melissa because she had Davian. Lottie hated Melissa because he was hers. Lottie hated Melissa because she was the one he went home to. Melissa did nothing to her. Or did she? Did Melissa find out and kill Lottie? Could it be? No. Lottie sounded here as if she was plotting something. *The person I hate the most is Davian. I want to hurt him the most.*

My phone goes off, causing me to jump. It's Lottie's mother.

'Wait, calm down, I can't hear you,' I say over the hysteria of tears and loud sobs.

'They are going to exhume her grave.'

My legs give way as I slump down on the chair. The room spins. I'm not sure if I heard her right.

'What?!'

'Oh, I don't know, as if this hasn't been painful enough.' She sniffs. 'The police came to let me know. Why can't they just let my baby rest in peace?'

Why dig out her grave? Didn't they have what they wanted from the autopsy? Something is new in the investigation. I wish I knew what.

'Apparently the police found something. They wouldn't tell me, of course.'

Her mum sobs again. Why is she telling me this?

'When are they are going to exhume her?' I ask.

'What?'

'When?'

'I think its tomorrow, why?'

'No reason.'

I do have a reason. I'm going to go to the cemetery and see for myself. After I put the phone down, I go to the bathroom. My cheeks are hollow and my eyes are hooded; signs of no sleep are showing now. I open the cabinet and pop two aspirins and wash them down with tap water.

The fridge is empty. I ran out of milk and bread. I sigh and put my hand through my hair. The police are digging out her grave. Lottie was buried just a few weeks ago. Why dig up the grave? What did they find?

Chapter Thirty-Two

Six feet under. Why that expression? Not from the Richmond Cemetery, where Lottie's coffin is buried under that soil. As if this hadn't been traumatising enough, now this? What possible reason have the police has to dig up her coffin? The police won't exhume the grave in broad daylight, so I go there when it starts to get dark.

I make out DC Gallagher in the distance. With my heart thumping in my mouth, I lurch towards a tree, not close enough, but not far enough. I climb up the tree and wait with a hoodie over my head to conceal myself. It's dark, but I'm not taking any chances.

There is another bloke with DC Gallagher, most probably the pathologist, who looks my age. There are three workers, from the cemetery I presume, and two people in white bodysuits, the forensics. There is a power shovel; in it is a man waiting and this is too upsetting. DC Gallagher says something to the one of the workers and the worker nods at the man inside the power shovel.

The leaves scamper in the wind, but the humming of the engine fades that out. I close my eyes shut, not wanting to see this, but I have to. I have to see Lottie's coffin rising back from the earth, not letting her rest in peace. If my mother were here to see this, she'd start to cross herself and pray. It seems blasphemous, against God, against nature. A chill runs down my spine. What are they doing? Disrupting the dead, toying with the order of things. This is not how it's supposed to happen, my friend being killed, buried, and then have her coffin dug up.

I grip my hand on the trunk tighter as the sound of the shovel echoes into the night. The coffin rises and the workers plus the forensics team get on with their work. A forensics van comes into view as the workers lift the coffin and take it inside the van and shut the door. DC Gallagher says something to the driver before it drives off.

I go into the kitchen, reach for the bottle of vodka and gulp on it, staring at the bag. I hear whispers; it's all in my head, but I hear that voice. Her voice hissing through the walls.

Come on, Anthony, break a leg. You made it this far. Are you going to give up now?

***

Lottie's Recordings. Clip Twenty-Two

I make a list of things to do. Why would I want to be with a man who is taking so long to act? Who's moody and distant? We have nothing in common except Anthony. We come from different planets. I put him on this high pedestal. In my eyes, he's the most beautiful man in the world with his soft features and blue eyes. Sadly, beauty fades; too bad his personality is a downer. Davian will never be mine, but I won't give up so easily. If I can't have him, that doesn't mean that someone else, or Melissa, can have him either.

Fuck her! Fuck him! Fuck them! Fuck them all. I hope they rot in hell. I don't care anymore.

***

I pause the video and go to the bathroom and wash my face. Why had she bought a gun? Davian said they had sex twice; she'd made it look like they were seeing each other on a regular basis. How to explain the Post-its? It's Davian's handwriting, I know it is. I have seen it enough to recognise how he writes the number eight, how he doesn't curl it all the way and the letter Y is always a capital letter. The big questions tear and punch at my brain. Why? How does all of this relate to her being murdered?

I have one video left and I have the ideal place to finish it.

Chapter Thirty-Three

The cabbie drops me three blocks away. After I pay him, I pull the hoodie over my head, holding the straps of my bag as I move across the road keeping my head low. The street is deserted, the orange lamp flickers. A cricket is singing, which makes the whole neighbourhood serene and peaceful. I glance at the brick buildings from across the street; most of the lights are off. Each apartment with its own tale and its own secret. It didn't look like a heinous crime had been committed in one of these apartments. It looks the same, unaffected by the whole experience as if nothing ever happened. Soon it will be up for rent again and someone else's things will replace all her belongings. How many times had I been there coming in and out without any care or consideration that it would be my last?

I cross the road with the paperclips ready. The communal door is open as always; nobody bothers to close it behind them. One time a neighbour got cross with me for closing the door.

I put on my gloves and nip inside. I don't take the lift. I keep my pace light to avoid being heard. I don't switch on the light. Instead, I use my phone flashlight and keep an eye on my footing. The flat is on the fourth floor and my heart stops when I see the barricade tape across her door. It seems surreal to see that tape on her door. How I'm going to get through the tape without removing it is beyond me. I'm not a big guy; maybe I can manoeuvre my way around it. I fiddle with the open paperclips. My hands are shaking as my shoulders tense. I'm about to break into the apartment of my dead friend. How many crimes had I committed these past few weeks? My forehead becomes moist as my hands work on the lock, being careful not to tear the tape. My ears open to each sound, but it's silent as death. I rub the nape of my neck and try to relax my shoulders. I won't be able to pick the lock if I don't stop fidgeting. A friend at school had taught me the trick to pick locks.

Click!

I remained perfectly still for a moment, staring at the door. I gently try to move between the tapes. My leg gets tangled and I lose my balance. I place my hand on the door and a bit of the tape tears.

Footsteps coming up the stairs.

I freeze.

'Shit,' I whisper, and conceal myself in the darkened corner.

I listen intently to the footsteps. They stop. I hold my breath. What if someone followed me here? Maybe the killer knows I would come here. I swallow the lump in my throat. A key in a lock. A door opens and closes. I take in a breath. I remove the tape that caught on my leg; nothing I can do about that. I don't turn on the light. I smell the strawberry-scented candle in the air. It's as if she's still living here. However, that scent is covered with something else, something I don't want to think about. Chemicals, bleach and death.

I see Lottie sitting on the white leather sofa talking on her phone. I can hear her laugh between the walls. I see Lottie walking from to room to room, raising her hand in the air while playing music. Her long dark wavy hair bouncing as she walked.

I start through the corridor as I hold my phone with trembling hands. I hear a laugh behind me. I jump. I close my eyes, shaking my head. She's gone, but her presence in here is alive and strong. I see her peering at me through the mirror on the dressing table. I stand in her bedroom, looking down at the mattress stripped of its sheets.

A chill rush through me. There is her desk in the corner where she must have recorded the videos.

I unzip my bag and lay the laptop in front of me on the carpet and she comes alive in front of me.

***

Lottie's Recordings. Clip Twenty-Three

All those months that I have wasted, months that I'll never get back. I went to see Davian today. He was rather grim; I grow tired of his mood swings. That's when I realised that he will never do it, he won't leave her, and it was a failed hope to bully me or tease me as he did in the beginning.

'I can't wait for you to make up your mind,' I said.

'Not now,' he said.

That was when I snapped. 'Yes, we do this now damn it! You will give me this chance to speak out. I have watched you for months and months. All that pain and heartache, crying myself to sleep.'

He stared at me softly, shaking his head. 'Lottie…'

'Don't you dare 'Lottie' me! I fucked up a relationship with a man who truly loved me for you. I, the fool, thought you were going to act, but why should I settle for a man who doesn't love me and will not love me back? I can't do this anymore going back and forth, wondering and hoping that maybe, maybe you will act on what you promised, but you won't. I can see that. It's just you jerking me around as you always have. You don't want to be with me.'

'So that's it? You're giving up.'

'Fuck you, Davian. I'm not giving up. You brought this on yourself. This is my way to tell you I don't want to be with you anymore. I don't want you, I don't want you near me, I don't want you to touch me, I don't want you to look at me. I can't bear it I can't take it. It hurts. Don't you get it that standing here looking at you, it hurts!'

He tried to take a step towards me, but I held out my hand and he stopped.

'It's over. We are done. I'm going to hand in my resignation to Giselle. In the meantime, forget everything. I don't want to see you ever again. You ruined me.'

I turned to leave. I felt a grip on my arm and I shook it away, but he pulled me to him.

'Wait!' he said, his eyes ablaze.

'Don't you get it? I'm done waiting for you.'

'Lottie, I'm going to Indonesia. I'm going to tell her there.'

'You're going to Indonesia? Good, stay there!'

I broke free from him.

'Don't do this, come on.'

'Goodbye.'

That's done now. It's time to get through the next items of the list. Everything must be perfect. One mistake and the whole thing can blow up in my face. I won't have him, but if he thinks he's free from me, he has another thing coming.

***

The screen goes black, and the silence envelopes the room. No, it can't be over… is that it? What does she mean with the items on her list? And what she said in the clip of her going to the apartment to end her non-existent affair with Davian. Everything must be perfect. One mistake and the whole thing can blow up in her face. What does it all mean? I check the date of the clip: two weeks before she died. Only unanswered questions. I jerk up as a sound comes from outside. Footsteps. Voices. Shit! I don't move as I listen. The voices are coming from outside the door.

'Why is most of the tape removed?' a woman asks.

Fuck. Fuck. Fuckety fuck.

I slam the laptop shut. I shove my phone in my pocket and scan the room. Where am I going to hide? The door opens. Shit! I crawl under the bed, holding the bag under me. Something is shining on the floor. The lock pick. I stretch out from under the bed, my heart drumming against my chest.

'Do you think someone has been here?' a man asks.

It's DC Gallagher and James. I reach for the lock pick and scrabble back under the bed, not making a sound, trying not to breathe.

Footsteps.

A pair of black pumps appear and I shut my eyes. *Please don't look under the bed. Please don't look under the bed.*

'Clear,' DC Gallagher shouts.

The shoes disappear from view.

'All clear,' he says.

They open something, a case by the sound of it, with latex gloves being put on.

'We've searched the place already,' James says.

'It's got to be somewhere,' DC Gallagher says.

Their voices are close now.

'The killer must have taken it and destroyed it,' James says.

'What sort of data does the laptop contain that got her killed for it?'

'Blackmail, I suppose.'

They think she got killed because she was holding information on her laptop. She did, but not what they are suspecting. I place my hand over my mouth, but my ears are on alert.

'We need to find something. So, we look again; something about this whole murder doesn't add up.'

'Yes, but I don't know what we are supposed to look for.'

'The whole thing seems odd...' DC Gallagher says. 'From the beginning, it didn't seem right. I told you this.'

'That whole thing was staged, yes.'

Does DC Gallagher think the murder was staged? How? Who would stage a murder?

'You saw the facts, so we look again just in case forensics missed something.'

How in the hell I'm going to get out of this? What if they look under the bed? Not only do they find what they are looking for, but I'm going to prison for a very long time.

'I still think we need to talk to Anthony again.'

I bury my hand in my mouth with the mention of my name.

'Why?'

'I don't know; he rubs me up the wrong way,' James says.

Am I a suspect?

'We can't arrest the kid for rubbing you up the wrong way. He is not a suspect, and you know that,' DC Gallagher reasons.

'Yeah, I know.'

'You saw the video footage of him at the exhibition. I need to get to the bottom of this. Davian swore he didn't have an affair with her. Just had sex with her a couple of times. Yes, his belongings were found here, but I don't know.'

'But his prints weren't on the gun. Even though I know you want to nail him, you can't,' DC Taylor says.

'Believe me, DC Taylor. I would love to nail that cold, good-looking son of a bitch,' DC Gallagher says.

'You really don't like him, do you?'

'No, I don't.'

The black pumps return. Oh God! I'm so busted. What was I thinking of coming here? At least I know now I am not a suspect. So that's good.

'There is something, though, something we are missing, and it might be right in front of our noses,' DC Gallagher adds. 'That's why we are here: to find something we might have missed.'

'When did you say you're going to hear back from the lab?'

'In three days.'

James whistles. 'The girl did spend a lot of money on exotic underwear.'

'Put that away!' DC Gallagher hisses at him.

More movements. What are they looking for?

'I'll take the kitchen,' DC Taylor announces.

DC Gallagher moves about and opens a door. Lottie's wardrobe by the sounds of it. Hangers moving.

The black pumps walk across the room. I see DC Gallagher only partially, with her hands on her hips. She must be desperate. This case is costing them a lot of money and time. I wish I could drop hints, but I can't. She keeps staring down at the floor and takes a few strides to the dresser. She runs her hand over the surface and crouches down.

I roll to my side even though DC Gallagher's back is to me. She looks under the dresser. My back is soaked with sweat. I clutch the backpack, pressing so hard my knuckles are turning white.

'DC Taylor!'

'What?'

She picks up something, holding it with her latexed thumb and forefinger. What did she find? I can't see, but it's small.

'Come here, I found something!'

Chapter Thirty-Four

'Is that a... spring?' DC Taylor asks.
'Looks like it.'
'Where did you find it?'
'Under the dresser.'
'Why would there be a spring?' DC Taylor asks.
'That's what I'd like to find out.'

I lay my face on the carpet, listening to the sounds. Latex gloves being removed. A briefcase slamming shut until silence envelops the room. They're gone. I lay there under the bed, my body paralysed. Lottie is there with me lying face down under the bed with me. Her face is half gone. The skin melted away, blood oozing out of it. I try to scream, but it's as if I'm underwater. I see her face restore itself to how it was. I try to move, but I can't, as if I woke up but my body is still asleep. I lift my head and bang it against the bed. I could lie here for a bit. Only for a bit.

It's morning when I crawl out from under the bed and rush out of there before someone sees me and calls the police. Questions burden my mind as I lumber out into the street. People are out, on their way to work, too preoccupied to notice the lad with a black hoodie and backpack walking past them. What to do next? I haven't solved anything. Shall I leave the laptop in the police station? I'm sure it will help DC Gallagher with more clues, but how am going to do that?

The flat above me is playing music. I enter the kitchen, light a cigarette and open the fridge. There is a carton of milk and a block of cheese. I sit down at the kitchen table with cheddar cheese for breakfast. I cut the cheese in chunks and pop it in my mouth. The taste melts on my tongue. I slide the laptop out of my backpack. Now that I know the information it has, I don't know what to do with it. I can't take it directly to the police, but I can leave it. I go back to the photos and Post-its. The only parts in those clips that were true are the night of Davian's exhibition and of the house. I haven't found who killed her. Maybe the police will, in time. I pick up the photo with the hearts again; I don't know for how long I sit there eating cheese and staring at it, trying to comprehend the meaning of it. Why was it in her bedroom at her parents'? It looks innocent; only a photo given as an apology. I put the photo down and light a cigarette. I switch on the lamp and rub my neck. I'm tired and sore. I'll give anything for a night of good sleep. I think of my next move. I don't have any. I mash the cigarette in the ashtray. There isn't much I can do but sleep, or try to. I switch off the lamp and switch it on again quickly. I glance at the photograph, face down. I switch off the lamp and turn it on again. Something is written on that photograph. I look in the cupboards. I'm sure I have a UV light somewhere. I open drawers and cupboards until I find it. I fumble with the switch when it does. I place it at the back of the photograph and the words become visible. Lottie had left a message, her final words.

Chapter Thirty-Five

There are different types of invisible inks and some become visible under hundred-watt lightbulbs, but the words become clearer under the UV light. Lottie had gone to great lengths, and for what? Because my friend didn't return her affections? Invisible ink can be easily made at home if you have the right ingredients. Onion or lemon juice, baking soda, and vinegar are a few. The words are chilling and shake me to my very core. All the things she didn't say in the clips are on the back of a photograph. A photo given by Davian and I had it in my possession all this time, but how could I have known? All I know is our friendship. Who I thought Lottie was, the kind of person she was, was a lie. Everything about her was a lie, so was our friendship. The real Lottie is here in this invisible ink.

I doubt this message will be found. I doubt anyone is clever enough to look closely at this photograph and put it under visible light where my words, my final words, are being said. The list is in order. I want Davian to read this, but he doesn't care. He never cared. I could have made him happy but he's so cold, so withdrawn from everything. The clips I recorded are partly lies. There was no affair. I have never been to the apartment in Chelsea, and there was no discussion of him ever leaving his beloved Melissa. We only had sex twice, at his exhibition and in the old house. He didn't want me, so I wanted to give him a hard time. The clips were a setup for Anthony. He was his friend, after all. He was the one that put a good word in with that bitch Giselle, so it's his fault too. I gave him my laptop containing video clips of me telling a few porky pies after his laptop broke down. His laptop was fine. I was the one who broke it. I forged Davian's handwriting. It was easy enough; the fool had left me a Post-it after we had sex. I made a copy before I gave it back to him to confiscate. I wrote a few Posts-it's with messages to make it look like there was something going on between Davian and I, took photos to make it look like there was something going on. I dumped Abdel because he irritated me. I didn't want to be with him anymore. Did he think he could dump me and come back? Fuck him. Fuck Anthony. Fuck Davian. Fuck everyone. Fuck you all. I bought a gun. Trying to hold the trigger with a spring is a bitch but practice makes perfect. The task was simple; I'll use a spring to make it look like I had been shot and stick it to Davian. Eat that, you pompous, cold-hearted son of a bitch. I hope you'll rot in hell.

It's like someone poured a bucket of ice-cold water all over me. It was a lie. All of this was for nothing. It was to set us all up. She wanted to ruin everything, her life, and take Davian and me along with her, for what? Because the guy had sex with her twice and refused to leave his girlfriend for her? All of this for Davian? Davian had cost her everything including, her life. She did it all for him.

My legs collapse under me. I slump on the chair. I stare ahead with my mouth parted. She actually… no… it can't be… no, no, no. It was an accident. Lottie didn't mean to get shot in the face. Something went horribly wrong. She only meant to wound herself and make it look like Davian had done it. The thought alone makes me sick. That explains the marks on the furniture DC Gallagher had found. Lottie was trying to make the gun stay in position, but with what, I don't know. How come the police didn't find this out? The spring DC Gallagher found under the dresser; it was for the trigger. Lottie must have practised with the unloaded gun but when it was loaded, everything went wrong. How did she even…? I rub my eyes.

Lottie planned all of this to its final detail: having dinner with Ella, the loud music to muffle the gunshot. She was insane. Her obsession was so deep and it was all for nothing. Lottie wasn't murdered. Her death was accidental. Her poor parents. They are the only people I feel sorry for. The bitch deserved what came to her. I was her friend. I loved and adored her. How could she do this to me? Setting me up and putting me in this position? All of this because I'm a friend of her unrequited love? How the hell am I going to get out of this. Who would believe me? I had to show this photograph with its invisible message to the police. They are chasing a non-existent killer. DC Gallagher said she had a feeling it was staged, and it was. I have to tell her, which will leave me in handcuffs.

Chapter Thirty-Six

I stand outside the police station, glancing up at the building. My breath rises and falls as I build up the courage to go inside and hand over the laptop and the most important item, the photograph. I try not to think about what could happen to me. I might be placed under arrest for withholding evidence from the police, but I have to clear Davian's name. This is what friends do. I frown at the pavement; would he do the same for me? I think he would. His life is ruined because of this. Lottie had her fun, now it's time to put an end to this. I'm scared, but not worried. DC Gallagher would work out the rest and she has a confession from Lottie herself saying all of this was one big charade. I take one long breath, hold it in, and step inside. I walk to the desk where a bored police officer in uniform is scribbling in a notebook.

'Yes?' he says, without looking at me.

'I would like to talk to DC Fiona Gallagher regarding Lottie Gibson's murder case.'

'And you are?' he asks.

I place the laptop on the desk. The police officer glances at it, then his eyes look up at me for the first time.

'What's that?' he asks.

'Tell her it's Anthony Hughes. I have Lottie's laptop and I have a lot of explaining to do.'

It's a blur after that. DC Gallagher is out, so I'm taken to a room to wait. I don't know for how long

I waited but it seemed like a while. DC Gallagher comes and I tell her everything, not leaving anything out. DC Gallagher and DC Taylor listen with serious expressions on their faces as they take notes. I beg them to look at the photograph. I don't think DC Gallagher knew what to do with me. Her eyes keep slicing through me, then they take me to a cell but not handcuffed. In the cell with me is a man dressed in a blue boiler suit, who sits on the bunk staring into space. I wonder what he did. I'm exhausted. All I want to do is lie down, but I want to stay awake so as not to miss a thing. My eyes are heavy and slowly I doze off.

When Lottie came over to my apartment to hand me the laptop, her face had a glow on it, her eyes clear and bright. She gave me a toothy grin, stepped inside, and placed the bag on the coffee table.

'Here you are,' she said.

'Really, you shouldn't,' I said.

'Oh, no need to worry. I don't use it that much anyway.'

'Thank you.'

'You're welcome. Oh, I have to go somewhere, but can we catch up soon?'

'I would love that.'

She came to me, took my hand to hers, and kissed me on the lips. The last time she stood so close to me was at the party. I was taken aback, but thrilled.

'You're a good friend, Anthony,' she said. 'You're a good everything.'

She kissed me again on the lips. 'We'll catch up soon and talk, okay?'

I nodded.

Little did I know it would be the last time I ever saw her. That she had already made up her mind. From the look on her face, the cheery expression, she didn't look like she was about to set us all up. That I was being set up, and that her kissing me, telling me I was a good friend, a good everything as she put it, was her way to say goodbye to me. She didn't plan to be shot and die, but she knew our friendship would never be the same. Even if her plan had worked, if she'd made it look like Davian had shot her and wounded her, I think the guilt, to live with that remorse of knowing what she had done, would have eaten her away.

A uniformed policeman wakes me up; the man in the blue boiler suit is gone. I'm taken back to another room for another interview. DC Gallagher and DC Taylor are there and this time, they are going to record everything. So again, I repeat everything. Careful not to leave anything out.

'We have read the message on the photograph,' DC Gallagher says.

I wait for her to go on.

'I knew something was off, but I couldn't put my finger on what exactly. We are looking through more things, but soon, the case will be closed.'

'And Davian is cleared?'

'Davian's name will be cleared,' she said. 'As for you, I need to see how to deal with this. Withholding evidence from the police is a crime, and what you did has wasted police time.'

'So I'm going to be charged.'

'I'll see what I can do, but no promises.'

I won't forget her; Lottie will never be far away from my thoughts. I'll never get to see her again. I will never see her face, her smile, the glow in her eyes. I will never get to hold her hand, feel the softness of her skin. Without her, there will always be an emptiness in my life. I will never be the same. She let the most stunning thing she had ever seen be the centre of her universe. She let her obsession break her and destroy her utterly and completely. It cost her life and we are suffering from the wreckage she has created. I look at the stone.

Lottie, you'll be loved always.

I hold the bouquet in my hand. If only she knew how I felt about her. What if I'd told her? Would she have reconsidered? She hated Davian so much she wanted to ruin his life, but I was supposed to be her friend. I loved her. Those questions, those what-ifs, will never be answered. She nearly took me down along with her. I wasn't charged for withholding evidence from the police, but I had to pay a hefty fine. Davian doesn't work for Giselle anymore, although she apologised and offered him back his position he politely declined. He and

Melissa had reconciled and he moved to Japan. He's working on his photography book and soon he'll have an exhibition over there. I wish him well. As for me, well, I no longer work for Giselle either. I can't stand to walk in the corridors Lottie has walked, to see the cubical where she once sat being occupied by someone else. I haven't figured out what to do, but I'm not worried. I glance at her grave once more and toss the bouquet of flowers in the bed of grass.

'I hope you're happy now, bitch. I hope it was all worth it.'

I need your help!

Thank you for reading The Secret She Kept! This book has been a joy to write, but writing a book is not as glamorous as it seems. When I'm typing the words with tried eyes, it's you who keep me going. Knowing that readers enjoy these stories brings a smile upon my face. If you enjoy what I write, you can help this little writer out by writing a review on Amazon or Goodreads or any platform of your choice. Reviews are the lifeline for authors and readers trust other readers. If you use social media, spread the word. It will be wonderful to have my book listed with others you have enjoyed.

You can sign up for my newsletter, and keep updated with new releases, offers, updates and giveaways.

https://joannewritesbooks.com

Other works by J.S Ellis

In Her words: One night, one man, one mystery

While she seems to have it all, Sophie Knight is looking for more. When gorgeous and carefree Michael Frisk walks into her life, he offers the excitement and passion she desires.

Sophie is willing to risk everything she has. After all, she is used to concealing things from her husband—like her alcoholism, her unhappiness. But soon she has more to hide. She wakes up one morning in an alcoholic haze and finds bruises on her body, but has no recollection of what happened to her. Was she raped?

When unsettling notes and mysterious phone calls start, Sophie wonders whom she should turn to. Is Michael the cause of the frightening things happening in her life, or is he the answer to her problems?

Theodore: The Neighbour's Cat.

My roommate is a serial killer.
And I have been powerless to stop him because I... am a cat.

Don't get me wrong, Dean has never been cruel to me. He provides me with shelter, toys, and plenty of affection. But I have seen his dark side, his brutal treatment of women, and I can't bear to watch anyone else get hurt.

Jane from next door is attractive for a human, not to mention being incredibly kind. That kindness may get her killed. I've seen how Dean looks at her, I know what he's plotting. In his mind, she's his for the taking. I wasn't able to save the others, but I'm not ready to give up. One way or another, I have to figure out how to communicate to Jane that she's in danger.

Can I find a way to warn her in time? Or will she become just another name on his growing list of victims?

The Rich Man: He's too good to be true or is he?

Her boyfriend vanished, but moving on could be murder...

Acey left without a word, leaving Elena alone to pick up the pieces of her broken heart. Determined not to be crushed by his betrayal, she forces herself to get over him.

Never did she fathom the unspeakable darkness closing in...

Sinclair Diamond breezes into her life like an answered prayer. Handsome. Wealthy. Charming. As he lovingly dotes on her, Elena finds herself falling for him.

But Sinclair has unspeakable secrets all his own.

Men in black suits trailing them. Shady business dealings. The odd chain of events surrounding his first wife's death. The more Elena learns about Sinclair, the more her apprehension builds. Yet when a ghost from her past reappears, Elena is forced to face a startling truth that could cost her everything.

Can she escape the web of deceit tightening around her? Or will she be the next to mysteriously disappear

Lost and Found Book 1

Despite being polar opposites, Phoebe and Adele's friendship has stretched on for years. One a bubbly blonde, the other raven-haired and studious. They seem to have nothing in common, yet the bond between them is unbreakable.

Or so Phoebe thought.

She never believed Adele would hide anything from her until she sees her sneaking off with her handsome neighbour. Feeling betrayed, Phoebe begins to see cracks in their friendship she never noticed before.

Then, Adele vanishes.

Fearing for Adele's safety, Phoebe searches for clues about her disappearance. However, the deeper she digs, the more she realizes she didn't know Adele as well as she thought. Yet as revelations come to light, one mystery remains. What happened to Adele? And how is her disappearance connected to the stranger next door?

Hide and Seek Book 2

Hope is waning with Phoebe no closer to finding her best friend, Adele. Her suspicions involving her neighbor, Alan, have been cleared, leaving her no other hunches to pursue.

Until the letter arrives.

A message, written in Adele's hand, paints a picture of a side of her friend's life Phoebe never knew. Renewed with optimism that she is still alive, Phoebe launches back into the investigation. Among the pages of Adele's communications Phoebe finds evidence pointing to an unlikely suspect...

And yet another connection to Alan.

He seemed so concerned about the investigation, wanting to help in any way he could. Was the man next door a genuine ally? Or working to protect the real culprit?

The Confidant

Secrets have deadly consequences.

A part of him knew she was always lying, but he could change that. He could change her.

When charismatic Zoë first sits in Jason's salon chair, he can immediately tell they have a connection. Who wouldn't? She was smart, witty, and incredibly funny, everything someone could want in a budding friendship. But soon, Jason learns there is more to Zoë than meets the eye.

When lies are uncovered and secrets exposed, Jason must decide just how far he's willing to go in the name of friendship.

How far should he go to uncover the truth? If he digs too deep, could Jason lose the very person he's trying to keep?

When it all comes crashing to the light, and someone's very life hangs in the balance, will he regret what he's done? Or will Jason wish he had only done more?

The Secret They Kept

Emily Clarke thought her dreams were coming true. Her business was thriving and she was moving into a beautiful new house. Yet this dream quickly morphed into a nightmare.

Rocks being thrown at her windows.
Haunting messages written on glass.
Items mysteriously disappearing.

Emily's nerves are on edge, which is only made worse by the man across the street constantly screaming at his wife. By befriending their son, Lucien, she learns a dark truth about the street she now calls home. Lucien has a brother who went missing ten years ago, as did the last occupant of Emily's house.

Emily wants to believe these ominous events are past history until her ex-boyfriend vanishes without a trace. Now, she's convinced she is a pawn in someone's twisted game.

Can she uncover who is behind these disappearances before becoming their next victim?

Scan the code to buy the books

About the author.

J.S Ellis is a thriller author. She has a degree in creative writing, English literature and digital marketing. She lives in Malta with her husband and their kitties, Eloise and Theo. When she's not writing or reading, she's either cooking, eating cheese and chocolate, or listening to good music and enjoying a glass of wine or two.

Website: https://joannewritesbooks.com
Facebookhttps://www.facebook.com/authorJ.SEllis
Instagram: @ author_j.sellis
Goodreads: http://bit.ly/2P8a9xx
Pinterest: https://bit.ly/3iqBvrU
Amazon: https://amzn.to/30rbKSq
Bingebooks:https://bingebooks.com/author/j-s-ellis
Bookbub: https://www.bookbub.com/authors/j-s-ellis

Made in the USA
Columbia, SC
17 October 2024